Bedlam

Bedlam

A Novel

Jennifer Higgie

VERSO
London • New York

This edition first published by Verso 2026
First published by Sternberg Press 2006

1 3 5 7 9 10 8 6 4 2

Verso
UK: 6 Meard Street, London W1F 0EG
US: 207 32nd Street, New York, NY 10016
versobooks.com

Verso is the imprint of New Left Books

ISBN-13: 978-1-83674-204-3
ISBN-13: 978-1-83674-206-7 (US EBK)
ISBN-13: 978-1-83674-205-0 (UK EBK)

British Library Cataloguing in Publication Data
A catalogue record for this book is available from the British Library

Library of Congress Cataloging-in-Publication Data
A catalog record for this book is available from the Library of Congress

Typeset in Electra LT by Hewer Text UK Ltd, Edinburgh
Printed and bound by CPI Group (UK) Ltd, Croydon, CR0 4YY

Bedlam

A NOVEL

Jennifer Higgie

For Martine Murray who made me go to Amorgos

Broadmoor Hospital, 1885

Perhaps it is the story that chooses the man and wraps him in it until he suffocates.

For me, it was the sun that made up my mind, and the sun became my story.

Despite the blood that persists in flowing through me, I am no longer the person I was born to be. I did not write my life, and therefore cannot tell you in simple terms what happened to effect such change.

I have left that task to the images that have fallen from my fingers since my youth.

I have let them fall, so that one day they might be picked up. My pictures describe me correctly.

I have laid my head on the grey sheets of Bedlam and was not allowed to leave.

I have dabbled in visions. This is the tiny image of me that the pinhole of people's minds has illuminated.

But what of before?

The fulcrum of my life took place when I was 25, the year I grew old and died as others knew me. It was the same year I discovered another realm, a place inhabiting a truth that is, I have been told, no more than an elaborate fiction.

Where have I come from to arrive at this place?

My recollection changes with every retelling.

For the moment, this is the story that slips from me.

London, July 1842

I have heard the heat there is so great it inhibits the singing of birds.

I have not slept for days. My head is filled with infinite lists. Sir Thomas speaks as if he were eating boiled eggs. As if they press hard against the inside flesh of his cheeks, against his tongue. Something must account for the way he forms his words. They meet resistance at every vowel and wobble into silence.

The sun, Richard. You will not believe the sun. You will have to struggle at first to accommodate it to your skin, to your appetite, to your palette.

My ignorance of sunlight gives him inordinate pleasure, and although I do agree with him on one count, that my flesh is more accustomed to rain than heat, I cannot look him in the eye because his assessment of my ability is so skewed. Namely, I know that struggle will be unnecessary in adapting such light to my palette. The idea of sun has been growing in me since I was born, like a bone growth that affects my every movement. If I have been so far deprived of the actual experience of it, except at its most pale and withered, I have not for a moment been deprived of dreaming. I have dreamt of light through a cloth, dripping through a wing. I have dreamt in yellow and gold. I have felt my sight singe my imagination. I have leapt into consciousness so hot I cannot breathe. It will be astonishing not to have to imagine such light, but to see and feel it, to move through and feel its presence in the architecture and the skin of the people it has chosen to live among.

My fingertips are restless and beg permission to begin.

They long to become active, to be things that undo in order to release something else: buttons, hard lines, colour, and the cloth that covers us. To collect tickets, shade eyes, dance with pencils. They will insist, I know, on revealing my skin, to let it swim.

I have never ridden a camel. I have never touched sand that did not lead to water. A language I do not speak has never surrounded me.

Will sweat change the colour of cloth I wear? Is Egyptian dust more difficult to remove from a collar, from a waistband, than the grime of Piccadilly?

Time

Finally. It is time. The clouds disappear and the sky heralds my future with unencumbered sunlight.

The sky smiles down at me.

The crowds at the dock resemble a flock of gulls fighting over fish.

My sisters and brothers are convinced I will come home dead or worse.

Arthur John has already inquired as to whether he will be allowed to join the rescue party, when I am made a slave.

Little John Alfred begins to sniff and rub his nose, Maria, resplendent in blue, droops. Her eyes are so wet and desperate I can hardly bear her presence. Recently, she has gazed too often at me with such a look.

She is growing so fast I find her hard to recognise. Fifteen. Her mind is too quick for her wits, for her body to keep pace. She trips herself up all the time. Her legs are no longer hers. She does not know how to occupy her hands. She tugs at her hair, distracted, until it comes out in thick, sad strings.

Sir Thomas pats her reassuringly and stresses she will not even notice her brother's departure. He will be back so soon.

My job is to be companion to Sir Thomas and to draw pictures for him of everything we will see.

Maria recoils from him.

I am used to her honesty, but flinch at his words for a different reason; my return is something so distant, so unasked for, I cannot imagine it. All of my energy is absorbed in my leaving.

Maria looks at Sir Thomas with opaque, bewildered eyes. She will not be patronised and presses closer to me. Sarah, cool Sarah, shakes her head and steps away, as if to distance herself from Maria's heat.

Are all families so formed of opposites as mine?

Maria clings to my arm like someone adrift.

Oh let him be, Maria. He will need to breathe if he is to embark.

Jane clicks her tongue in annoyance. Maria glares at Jane, averts her face and clings all the harder. I wink at Jane. She looks at me with lowered lids and sighs through thin lips. Sarah adjusts her bonnet, rearranges an invisible hair and rolls her eyes. I cannot bear their dreadful primness and touch Maria's elbow. It is hot and her skin is twitching.

The blue of her dress shines like a bruise.

Father's face is a welcome distraction from my bickering sisters.

He looks at me as if he cannot hear them.

His pride makes my throat sting.

Kisses. The tears of the girls, in varying degrees of intensity, their faces averted behind depressed dark curls. All except Maria, of course, who looks at me as if I were a drink and she a thirsty man.

Maria Maria.

Her hot worried hand slips into mine, and her lips approach my ear.

I feel the hair lift lightly from the skin at my temple at her closeness.

Her voice is as quiet as a sigh.

Richard. Perhaps you should reconsider.

I pull away from her and admonish her softly.

Maria! Please, do not do this to me. Not now.

I will not listen to her.

Father gazes at us with curious eyes.

She has irritated me with her darkness, but knows me too well, and, sensing my displeasure, swallows and attempts a smile instead.

I stroke her cheek.

My arms feel stiff in their new coat.

Good girl, I say, and hold her hand until it cools. When I return you will laugh at yourself.

She arranges her eyes and gazes at me, her face blank and hard.

I turn away from her.

A handshake with father, his good, glowing face. Maria puts her hand in my pocket.

She feels like a stone inside me. She will not let me leave. She would drown me in the bay with herself in the sack.

Father takes my one hand in his two and holds it tight.

I wait for your letters, Richard.

If you have to wait too long, father, it will not be my fault. You must remember this: the horse must have fallen, the boat sunk.

We laugh.

He wraps an arm around my shoulder and I breathe him like a child and turn to John Alfred who is begging to know if a ship is faster than a galloping horse.

Much faster, I say. He looks at me in awe, then away, and scratches his nose.

Faster than a train? He scratches harder.

Don't scratch! barks Jane and slaps his hand away from his face.

He glares at her and looks to me for an answer. We are all silent a moment.

John Alfred? I say quietly.

He will not say a word. He will no longer look at me. I talk to the side of his face, quietly, so only he will hear.

John Alfred, a ship is much faster. A ship has the wind to thank. A ship does not need a road.

He turns and beams at me. I see Jane's hand twitch. A drop of blood colours his nose. He wipes it away with the back of his hand.

Suddenly, everyone speaks their goodbyes.

Departure has ceased to be an idea.

The noise of that farewell! Hundreds of feet stamping up the gangway, the creaking and blowing and shouting of porters and horns, the sobs of girls with sailors, the awful brave faces of my fractured family way below me as we, Sir Thomas and I, lean on a rail and wave. Jane with her mother's eyes, Maria and Sarah so little, so opposed, so clutching as they strain their faces upwards and shake their small white hands so hard the air might snap their fingers. The boys with their mouths open, thunderstruck and envious of the size of the ship that will take their brother away.

Father's presence wrapped around them like a cloak.

All of their eyes linked in a common destination me.

And mine turned towards one I do not know.

I am full of unborn images.

It is only a matter of miles before they will begin to assume shape. Pictures almost resident in my head. Paintings almost glazed upon a wall.

The First Room

The ship is released, slips away, bellows. Faces stained with leave-taking avert naked eyes.

We retreat to our cabins, to wash, to prepare for supper, to regain the expressions we wore before such emotion made its mark. Sir Thomas has a cabin next to mine.

Meet you in an hour, Richard? In the saloon?

Our doors slam, the room sways, a cup jiggles on a saucer. I whistle.

My head is as light as a single hair. I could dance with anticipation.

A bed with a small rail. I have never so immediately loved such a small room. A dear, round window. It is like seeing the world through a looking glass. Seagulls enter and leave its circumference, flung about like scraps of paper.

I shall take an image specimen of the ocean and the birds and hide it away. I may need an ocean when I find myself in the desert.

I am dizzy with exhaustion. I am a poor man given a gift, plucked from the gloom.

The ship ploughs its way towards my pictures.

The cold grey sea never looked more like a blank thing. It could have been built to take me away, so I will be able to see the things inside my head waiting to be released.

A Child Talks of Death

I walk fast along the deck, the sea wind pouring into me and lifting me high. Birds float below the clouds. I have a belly full of breakfast and do not know what I shall see at any given moment. I fairly crackle with the energy of it all, and laugh out loud.

I catch a ball that appears in the air in front of me. It is hotly pursued by a small bundle of a boy, who stops abruptly and gazes at my new possession.

An imperious voice issues forth from his tiny, fat mouth. His hair flies up.

It is mine. Give it back.

There is something arresting about this child. Perhaps it is his rather old eyes.

I look into them, and they look into mine, filled with fury.

Tell me why I should give you this ball.

Without hesitation he replies if you don't, I shall have you killed.

I am taken aback.

By whom?

By my minions.

Oh. And how shall they kill me?

Some with guns and some perhaps with swords. One or two may employ cross-bows. It will hurt. Now give it back.

I hold onto the ball a little longer.

It is wrong to kill. Where is your mother.

He is impatient with me, and bored now.

It is not so wrong. You, sir, have done me an injustice. My mother is resting. Where is yours?

A good question. I think for a moment.

I am a motherless man and you are not God. Only God has permission to give or take lives.

He rolls his eyes. Kings kill lots of people and they are not Gods. And anyway, no man is motherless.

My mother died. And you are not a king.

How did she die? And how do you know I am not a king?

I pause. This is not a straightforward child.

God wanted her by his side. And you are too short for a king.

I silently hand him his ball back, and he begins, indifferently now, to bounce it.

He calls back over his shoulder, I shall spare your life, this once only. I thank him, gravely.

Sea Travel

I have looked so hard at the exterior of ships that being inside one is like entering a body, or a sculpture, or the mind of someone you have admired from afar. My cabin is the revelation of a secret. I feel more myself than I have in months. Perhaps it is the sharp clean air, which has spring-cleaned my head and lungs, washed away the accumulation of too much talk in too many smoky rooms. Or perhaps it is the reassuring instability that accompanies every moment, the groaning deck and the creaking, straining sounds of the sail. It is as if a large, benevolent beast had decided to facilitate our movement from one point to another.

A ship is somnambulant, for all its apparent function, conjuring reveries in its movement towards land, hinting at stories one can only guess at. A ship is stained with the grip of infinite travelling hands and the perfumed grime of infinite ports.

So much pleasure is to be had in this floating village: the sliding plates at mealtimes, the necessities of one choosing each step in a considered and balanced fashion. The look of concentration on a man's face as he walks towards me swaying; the way women's dresses billow in the wind, as their arms curve in futile attempts to secure hats to heads.

The absurd sight of men taking control via elbows, books, meal orders. A stray curl whipping a red cheek.

I am leaving, I have left.

My family is gone from the port and I, however briefly, from their lives. I have never been without them before.

They will grow without me. Of their own accord and in a brief few months, their height will increase and they will form opinions, the provenance of which I will be ignorant.

All will change except father. He is more permanent to me than a rock.

My father will never not be my father and I will never not know him.

Beneath us are invisible fish and sea beasts. My hands will not be still in their attempt to place on paper what I have not seen.

I have tried to draw the idea of fish. It has amused me no end.

These are not sketches I would show to Sir Thomas. He would sniff out their apparent lack of gravitas. Although we have seemingly talked at length about painting, for all intents and purposes we may as well have remained silent. Our talk is richer and more real when we discuss our respective families and the details of our journey.

He is a kind man, if a little pompous.

Travelling with him will assist me in developing a rich internal world.

My lips taste deliciously of salt as I direct my pencil towards its destination.

A Family

Walking into the breakfast room, I once again encounter the small boy, but without his ball and accompanied by a lady I assume to be his mama. He points at me and says loudly, That is the man who took my ball, mama. But I spared him.

People turn and stare. I am embarrassed, revealed to all as a ball-thief. I open my mouth but am silent. I cannot think of anything to say, but am saved by the lady, who smiles at me.

She has a warm face and small, dark-lashed eyes. A mossy green hat like something growing.

Hush, Tom. I am sure the gentleman did not mean to steal your ball. She looks directly at me, and faint dimples appear in her cheeks.

Unless perhaps you did?

Such a hat, such eyes!

I'm afraid, madam, I stand guilty as charged. I did steal the ball.

I planned to sell it and make a tidy profit.

We both laugh. Tom does not.

Mama, Papa is waiting. I am hungry.

Another smile. Excuse me. A glare from Tom.

I bow.

I watch her walk into the dining room and sit beside a man with a large, red beard, who glances at her, before resuming his scrutiny of a newspaper.

She murmurs something to him, he murmurs back and touches her hand.

She reaches for a teacup.

The boat lurches, her hand returns to her husband's, and I stumble slightly.

Tom is suddenly a little boy and clings to her arm. She gently takes his hand.

They are a family. Three people sitting at a table, holding hands as a ship sways and plunges.

When all is once again calm, they laugh, look at each other, and laugh again.

Then she fills her teacup and pours some milk for Tom.

He sips it with a satisfied face.

I do not know why, but the sight of it is enough to make me weep.

Disorientation

I cannot guess at what a sustained sea voyage would do to one's sense of orientation. I have been afloat only a few days, and, although out of sight, the earth is close enough for reassurance, in the untired birds, in the knowledge of imminent arrival, in the memory of recent departure. But to travel to the other side of the world, to not see land for months, to be suspended between the most transient, the most unstable of elements! I would like to try it one day, to see the pictures such detachment from the earth would force into my head and out of my hand. I would like to learn to use the stars as maps. I know it would change the way I hold my pencil. It would change the way I looked at the world, the way I walked across land. It would change my relationship to the night. I would need to navigate by the moon.

It is appropriate we are on water. As if we are nowhere and everywhere, as if what will happen will happen soon.

The coast reveals itself like a rabbit from a top hat. We crowd the stern to watch its arrival, to greet it. Men give their hands permission to be foolish, and wave like children at nothing that can respond. Ladies sigh and lean and gaze.

How lovely their dresses are, when they swell in the wind. I wonder if one has ever caused a woman to float away.

Women, to my mind, are even more mysterious than ships.

The seagulls sing their song of arrival, fly up from the decks and descend sharply into the waves. It is impossible to imagine the fear that inhabits fish at the thought of such attack.

Imagine the beak flashing through the waves, glittering, determined and blurred.

Imagine the dull clack and snap of its bite.

It is too terrible to countenance.

I would not wish the fate of a fish eaten by a bird on my worst enemy. Had I one.

Ostend

A place of fish smells and varnish beneath a thin, grey sky. Of flat, dull bread and desolate, nagging birds. Of inscrutable fishermen in clumsy wooden clogs and wide blue trousers that seem to flap even when the men are inside, seated at the long brown tables this place supplies so well. The older women have flat faces and swollen, floury bodies. But the young girls, with their soft, bright eyes and their skin like apricots and hard eggs, I could almost nibble. They have delicious sturdy waists and busy strong hands. The boys are cleaner than any boys I have ever seen, with shining eyes. Perhaps it is the wind or the omnipresent rain that washes them so effectively. Or perhaps it is the clean presence of their God, who would appear to be a simple man of few words and fewer opinions. Their churches are plain and scrubbed, which is right for such a place.

I was so little when I first saw a live fish. My father held me by the hand and we walked by the river. My mama was just dead. My father was quiet as was I. I do not know what he was thinking. I was thinking about my mama going to heaven and searched the sky for a ladder. I was worried. Mama was so weak and tired, now she was dead, how would she ever climb so high?

We silently threw stones into the water and looked down and saw a small thin fish trapped beneath a rock. I crouched and saw its eyes fixed on nothing, like tiny swollen raisins. My father lifted the rock and the fish swam away. I did not think of my mother then, watching that fish depart.

It shone in escape.

My father looked up at the sky and then at the water and he held my hand and we both laughed as the fish disappeared away from us, down the brightly shining river.

Where were my brothers and sisters then?

Who was holding their hands?

I do not know.

Increasingly I have no memory of occasions I should recall.

Scenes leak from my mind and find solace in my skin, a kinder, warmer place. Occasionally they erupt in me, beyond my control, and flow like lava, heating everything I have ever felt.

I do believe there are things that affect me, of my own making, which I cannot name. As if they live in me, and around me, but are ungraspable.

The people here speak like underwater creatures, in murmurs and gargles. They rarely smile, but when they do, I believe they do so truthfully. But it is also possible to imagine these lowland people living even lower, beneath the earth for a while. Perhaps it has something to do with the way they seem to be perpetually blinking in surprise, as if they had only recently emerged into daylight. They are earthbound, obviously in love with the colour brown and all of its cousins, despite their apparent affinity with water.

They fish for a living and are clearly at home on the sea, but the colour of the sea, even at its most grim, does not spring to mind when I think of them. It is perhaps significant that it is rare to find a painting of the sea here. All that I have so far witnessed appears to be preoccupied with interiors or tables. These images often depict rooms that throb with an atmosphere of recent departure. If you listen very hard you can almost hear the squeak and slam of a door, then the sudden silence of an empty room.

Perhaps the people here have assumed the guise of fishermen. And if so, who are they truly?

I wonder who dug them up, who washed them so well.

A Woman Who Weeps and Speaks English

Walking along a narrow path along the shorefront with Sir Thomas, we come across an elegant woman, sitting on a low wooden chair outside a small cottage. She is quite openly weeping.

We slow down as we approach her, and do not know what to do. She is wearing a dress of silver grey. Her hair is loose and brown.

Sir Thomas coughs and looks about nervously. I imitate him. I can think of nothing better to do.

She is impossible to ignore. The path leads almost directly to her, before veering away.

I assume she is a widow and is weeping at her loss. She is not weeping like a woman who has misplaced a trinket or broken a cup.

We are obliged to stop. She looks up at us and hiccups. She has narrow, pale hands and holds one to her mouth. A thin gold ring shines softly beneath a knuckle. She is panting slightly.

We keep looking at her, as we have no better plan. Then Sir Thomas speaks loudly, as is his wont with foreigners.

Madam. Do you speak English? May we be of assistance?

She holds his gaze with wet eyes.

I speak English.

Her voice is low, her accent difficult to place. French perhaps?

I do not need your help. But thank you.

Sir Thomas shifts awkwardly on his feet. I look at her face. She looks haunted. I speak foolishly, as if the sound of my words might aid her recovery.

Can we do anything? Surely.

She almost laughs and looks at her feet.

No. Thank you. Really, you are kind people.

And hiccups again.

I feel uncomfortable at that. I do not think Sir Thomas and I are especially kind. We merely stopped because the path was narrow, and a woman was weeping.

We nod stiffly, and move on, impotent.

The sea moves beyond us like a sodden brown handkerchief.

I look back at the woman. She has stopped her crying and sits very still and quiet gazing at the sea.

Sometimes grief rejects words like a river sinks boats.

Supper and Painting

Every evening we dine simply off fish, boiled well with potatoes and washed down with harsh ale. Sir Thomas busies himself after supper with letter writing, after telling me, in no uncertain terms, about who and what these people are. He treats me at once like a student, an honoured servant and even, after drinking, a friend, despite the fact that conversation with him often culminates in a rebuke. An example: these lowland people are, according to his logic, good, unimaginative, god-fearing and hard-working people, but could not be poets because the light is wrong, the presence of fish too pervasive.

But Sir Thomas, I ask him in all candour, with how many of these people have you spoken?

He pulls himself up slightly in his chair and stands, his cheeks suffused with a slight red wash.

I have been here before, Richard. I know this country. People are the product of their locale. Their land forms their minds as surely as a mother gives birth to their bodies. It is a flat land. Where is the spirit of art in these buildings, Richard? Where is the undulation in their thinking? When you see the Venetians you will understand how Art must reflect the world outside the window of the artist. There is no light here to speak of, Richard. There is no light.

He is breathless from such a speech. I search my pockets for a pencil. Surely he must intend for me to take notes?

I struggle with his logic, according to which I should make paintings that reflect Chatham's damp air and heavy earth.

I remember:

I am small and full of thoughts.

I ask my father: what will happen to me when I am grown?

He pauses.

Whatever you choose. An occupation that suits your temperament.

A wife. A family.

And if I choose to be something that does not yet exist?

He thinks seriously for a moment and then laughs.

Well then, Richard, you will bring it into being.

Before I could question Sir Thomas further, he retired to his room, his corpulent body moving with some efficiency out of the door. His absence filled the room pleasantly, and left me time to contemplate a painting on the wall of the communal sitting room. Sir Thomas could not have felt justified in his comments if he had really looked at it. Such a plain little painting, but so replete with things unsaid. Practically pulsating.

A fish, but such a fish! Scales like a robe, sad eyes full of sea. Why, this fish is so perfect it must have wriggled its way onto the canvas! How the elements in it glow: a lemon, so sour I shiver; a thin, thin glass filled with cold wine; a crisp white cloth; and three walnuts, all set against a deep dark background.

I gaze at it for a long time, and find myself perplexed. I do not know why.

Perhaps it is the skill with which the painter communicated the painting's most compelling paradox, namely that a close description of the real world often emphasises how unreal it is. The fish somehow more than the sum of its fishiness! A meal that will never be eaten!

A meal that may not have ever existed, here before me more alive than the chairs I can touch.

I do believe that this is what a painter should be doing, presenting the world back to itself, minutely observed, yet also imagined and so altered.

I would have liked to take this painting with me, as a constant reminder of how complicated a nut might appear to someone who might look upon one with an unbiased mind.

My room is small and clean and satisfyingly foreign. I fall asleep to the tug and push of waves on shingle.

In a Coach

The next morning, Sir Thomas, sombrely attired with a dark coat and a grim expression, treats me like a slightly backward student he may have met once a few years earlier.

Come boy, it is time to leave.

Of course, sir. Yes, I am ready.

You have remembered everything?

Yes. I think so.

He sighs.

Richard, merely thinking is never enough. We will never return to this place. Do you know, for a fact, that you have everything?

I look at the earth. It holds me in a solid, friendly fashion.

Of course, Sir Thomas, you are right. I am sorry. I do know, for a fact, that I have everything. I have looked beneath my bed and in the cupboards. I can assure you, sir, I have left nothing behind.

He sniffs.

Well then. Let us depart.

I nod.

The horses groan.

And so, we leave.

In deference, I become silent and respectful, pausing only momentarily on our way out of that convivial inn to secretly wave goodbye to my small friend, the fish.

We settle into our carriage like a couple of old women. I cluck over Sir Thomas and he begins to warm to me once again. He begins to hint that I may once again be filled with potential.

I am sure I glow.

It takes so long to reach our next destination. I cannot imagine how many decades it might take us to reach the other side of Europe.

To imagine standing on the banks of the Nile is to try and imagine floating upwards, through the air, to a place beyond the sky.

The countryside is monotonous, the conversation even more so. The roads are bad. After an hour we are groaning with backache. Reading is impossible, the words leap about so, and Sir Thomas is too enthusiastic in his opinions for any real exchange of ideas.

We stop for lunch in a small inn in a village flanked with forests. It is clean and friendly. An elderly woman with collapsing curls and a thin mouth brings us bread and cheese and wine. It is so plain every separate taste sings. The woman speaks a little English and is proud of the fact. She asks me where I am from. I tell her Chatham and London. From England.

She asks, is Chatham lovely?

It is very strange to hear the word Chatham in a foreign place.

I reply that it is not.

She looks a little disappointed and so I add 'but there are many ships'.

She looks satisfied at that, and fills my glass with wine

while Sir Thomas wrestles with a button on the sleeve of his coat, cursing.

I feel obliged to compliment on her village of choice.

You have a fine inn here. And your village is charming.

She looks at the floor with pride, then speaks quietly.

Yes. We have good spirits here.

Sir Thomas snorts.

I am taken aback.

What kind of spirits?

A man at the next table calls out impatiently for service, and so she nods to me and leaves our conversation adrift.

I feel an urgent need to know.

What spirits?

But the woman disappears into the kitchen and we do not see her again.

Back on the road, I long for air, and would like to travel with the door open, to hang my head out of this cramped space and breathe in the strange light that unifies such tedious countryside. In truth, I would like to be attached to a large balloon and be pulled along behind the carriage, and hear Sir Thomas' thin alto from a long, long way away.

His questions are interminable.

I gaze out at trees and look for good spirits.

I do not see any.

Richard, how would you best render that brown?

Tell me, Richard, of your assessment of your teachers at the Academy.

Richard, what criteria do you employ to choose your images out of so many available passages from Shakespeare's plays?

Richard, do let me tell you an anecdote about my sister's youngest child.

Richard, I tell you, that coachman is a scoundrel. Don't ask me how I know, I have more experience than you in these matters.

Richard, keep your eyes trained on our luggage, if you can. I know it is on the roof, but do your best. Can you not strain your neck a little further to see out a little more clearly? He may have an accomplice tucked away somewhere. He may have hidden him behind our cases.

Oh Richard, please do not look so sceptical. You are an artist, Richard. I know you feel the world keenly.

Oh Richard, are you awake?

Richard, is your energy fading? Are you tired, Richard? We shall be stopping soon. Why, you are pale, Richard, while I am as robust as the moment of our departure.

Much laughter.

Ad infinitum.

A painting, I feel suddenly like shouting, is no more than a suggestion, a product of the imagination expressing itself truthfully, and is never, except in its crudest manifestations, a lecture.

But I do not utter a word.

His voice increases in intensity as night begins to fall, as if he must convince himself, via me, of his lack of exhaustion, his capacity for being interesting. We are surrounded by darkness, bounced about like two stale loaves in a widow's basket.

I cannot sleep yet do not want to stay awake. I choose, instead, to look upwards, and watch, with tired eyes, the stars die.

I begin to hallucinate beds.

First Night in Germany

Dumb and sightless with exhaustion we stumble into some nameless inn, a dimly lit place in a tiny village. Not a dog barks, not a word of welcome is uttered. An old man staggers out sighing to meet us and carries our cases inside. I am too far gone to assist him and feel his resentment of my youth and empty hands. I do not care. I am beyond compassion. Sir Thomas has finally, wonderfully, lost the power of speech. We do not wash before our meal, we are too feeble and too hungry. Sir Thomas is almost white with tiredness and a little ashamed of his defeat as a result.

I silently give thanks to the spirits responsible.

We are fed by a woman whose face I forget as soon as she has placed our soup in front of us. Two men argue in hisses at the next table.

I do not understand a word they are saying, but their eyes, which thrust themselves occasionally in our direction, are full of vitriol. The soup is watery, none too hot, and punctuated with the occasional thin hair.

I eat like a sleepwalker, my back still trembling to the rhythm of the coach. My face has another skin, stuck with foreign dust and unuttered words.

I can hardly lift my head and take it to my room. I do not remember saying goodnight to anyone.

All I notice is that everything in my room is wood, except me. My flesh shines pink in the moonlight before it slips into darkness.

The Feeling When You Are Almost Awake in Another Country

Is it possible birds sing in different languages? I do not recognise the muffled song that floats into my sleepy head. The wind sounds hollow. My room is clean and bright. I have no memory of it from the night before. All I remember is my aching back, which has decided to stay with me. My bones are sore, my muscles stiff. I could sleep for a week. A tree knocks on the window. I hear faint, affectionate, masculine mumbling. I think it is a man with cows. I cannot help but wake up now. I hear words I do not understand and am filled with the thrill of incomprehension.

I am in a country I have never slept in before.

Now a knock on my door and not a tree but a girl with eyes so low I cannot see their colour enters my room and takes my water jug and fills it with water from a pail. Her hands are quick and red. She has obviously filled many a water jug in her time. Her yellow hair is covered with a white cap. She murmurs something I cannot understand. I am filled with a sudden urge to ask her about her family, to have her look at me. But I do not know how to begin conversation with this girl, the likes of whom I have never encountered before, and sink back into my pillows. My tongue crowds my mouth. I watch the slow movements of her back, which is broad and round-shouldered, and wonder what she must think of me, if she thinks of me at all. A foreigner in his night shirt, not much older than she is, and still in bed so late in the morning, staring at her. Her large behind moves from side to side beneath her dress, and comes to a stop, wobbling.

What is your name?

My voice startles me.

She turns and looks away, blushing, silent.

Why will women so rarely speak truthfully with men?

I persist.

Do you speak English.

She shakes her head and refuses to look at me. I am irritated by her coyness, but after some thought have to admit that I would not like my sisters in such close proximity to me if I were not their brother.

Brothers and sisters. Each one different from the other. None of them in most likelihood the person I assume them to be.

I reverse the thought: what do they know of me?

They know me only by the words I have spoken in their presence, and by the movements that have propelled me around them. But I am, of course, and in all modesty, so much more than I appear to be. As they are. But what remains if you strip a man of his words and his body?

Do they question this too? What is left of me when I am not with them? Do they doubt their knowledge of me?

I am sure they do not. They behave towards me as if they own me, and that such possession is a god-given right. But knowledge and ownership is, of course, more than proximity and biology.

Where, for example, do they travel when they sleep? And who, in their true hearts, would they like to touch?

I do not know. Except for Maria.

Everything is different every day, but still Maria and I talk to each other's heart, without acknowledgement.

We are often silent together. Such silence makes other girls, and in particular other sisters, appear shrill.

But then, sometimes they could be shouting, but I would not hear them. Without a doubt, at this point in time, right now, unless she is sleeping, Maria will be looking very hard at something and thinking about it.

However insignificant the object of her attention, Maria's gaze will always transform it into something magical.

It is a thought I find reassuring.

But I am in a foreign room. I will not let myself forget this. I will not travel backwards.

Memories can be terrible transporters.

This solemn girl clutching a water jug, this girl who I have already forgotten and who I do not know, slams the door on her way out. She still does not look at me.

She is not my sister and does not care for me.

My bed is warm and soft, and I slip down between unfamiliar sheets and am swallowed by a large foreign animal.

I think about kissing that girl whose eyes I cannot see. I imagine her small soft tongue on my silent one, her fat round breasts in my hands. She would whisper to me and I would not understand her. The thought is intense and unsettling.

I shake myself and stretch and my dream tumbles on top of me, as sudden as an avalanche, as clear and as awful as when I was asleep.

In my dream Maria is crying and crying, standing in the middle of a sunny, empty room. I walk up to her, to hold her, to comfort her, but she does not see me, and I am aware that five men have cursed her and must be dealt with if she is to be free. I ask them to leave, so I might speak to my sister. They do not reply. I am filled with rage. Maria cries all the more loudly. I grab hold of her hand and pull her towards me, but her hand falls apart and disappears, and I am in a river floating towards the sun that is so bright I assume it will explode. But I do not mind the thought. I am so happy to be away from that dreadful room that I cry into the gentle tide as I stagger ashore. The sun dries my tears.

I am hot and alone. Maria is nowhere to be seen. I know the men are dead.

Another knock on the door rescues me. A loud knock this one, from an apparently large fist.

Richard, are you awake?

I am, Sir Thomas.

Good lad. Sleep well?

He shouts as if he were waking me from a midnight sleep, a thousand miles from where he is standing. I laugh into my pillow and cough.

Thank you, Sir Thomas, very well. And you?

Like the dead, boy, like the dead.

Much laughter through the door.

It is time for breakfast, Richard, time to eat. Please hurry up.

I imagine him with his hands cupped against the wood of the door, spraying the cupola of his fingers with spittle.

I will be with you, Sir Thomas, I will be with you. Allow me ten minutes. Ten minutes, boy. We must be going. Yes. We must be going.

An Alpine Way

The horses pant and strain as the road becomes more and more steep. We are tilted back against the seats as surely as if a boy were holding our feet high. We have left the long, brown road of the Rhine behind us. I have memorised the ambiguous beauty of its castles. We are alone in the carriage. It is difficult to sense the countryside we are travelling through because the windows are too thick with grime. The sky is obscured by mountains grown dim with dust.

You will feel like a young Apollo, Richard, when we have scaled these heights. You will feel like Apollo both in body and in mind. For a mountain, Richard, is like a poem that has lifted your body high into the sky.

Sir Thomas blushes at his sensitivity and modestly lowers his eyes.

These mountains, he continues in a hushed voice, will prepare you for the heights I know you will ascend on your return, Richard, those artistic heights we all know you will not disappoint us with.

Us? Who else is sitting in this carriage? I look about me. As far as I can still see, it is only Sir Thomas and I in the carriage, but his comment has filled me with an anxiety I cannot name.

I smile weakly at him and say nothing. My toes press against my shoe leather. I pinch myself hard on my arm beneath my coat sleeve.

Inspiration boy. Inspiration. Spring is on its way! You are in the spring-time of your life boy, so much to grow in that head of yours!

Are you inspired, Richard? Are you ready to be elevated? Sir Thomas is over-excited. I counter-attack.

Sir Thomas, do please tell me the story of your first visit here.

Was it springtime, when you first visited the Continent?

He laughs out loud, happy at my question.

My dear Richard, it was not spring, but autumn! My trip had been delayed, but in hindsight, it was a blessing. The colours, Richard! The colours! I read verse in a forest!

I am allowed once more to retreat inside myself as his story continues. It is interminable and soothing, and demands nothing of me but the occasional admiring eye contact and head nodding.

A painting is not a mountain. Nothing is more paralysing to me than the idea that a picture is something to scale. A picture is something to be crept into, peeled back, dug away, clothed, undressed and dreamt. There are no mountains to be scaled in my pictures; they are places to hide in.

A New Place to Sleep

Our inn, which we reach after what seems to be an eternity of horse changes, precipices, staring strangers, claustrophobia, hunger, backache, tedium and unfamiliar languages, is more to my mind like the Idea of an inn than an actual inn. How is it possible that every splinter of wood, every blade of grass has been washed? Every pebble polished? Every breeze dusted down before it was allowed to blow so freely? Waking up here is like stepping into a story I do not understand. Although a good imitator of humanness, this alien author had not been properly informed of how grubby we human beings really are. I look everywhere for a sign that warns: enter this place and be filled with the scents and sounds and surfaces of a world that bears an uncanny similarity to the real world we think we recognise so easily, but is, in fact, a beautiful fraud. I could not paint such a place. Such beauty is somehow inaccurate. I would be called a liar, a sentimentalist, an idealist, and that would not do.

Mountains, the tips of which are touched with a faint white brush, frame the sloping roof of our inn, which was built to facilitate the removal of snow in winter. I cannot imagine snow in such a place, surrounded as we are with such growth and such gentle sunshine.

An Exercise

An exercise: I have decided that I will try not to think about anything that does not present itself to my immediate eye. My head is tired of travelling back and forward, in and out of memories. It is difficult to halt a conversation one is having with oneself. Instead, I will deflect the energy of these exchanges; I will become a better observer.

I will learn to understand the world by examining it more closely.

The rest will follow. It must. Where else could it go?

I want simply to observe the different shapes of petals and the muted colours of leaves. To spy on the occasional deer that stares at us through pine trees. To notice how the mouths of girls form their words differently from the mouths of boys. How the old men scratch their eyebrows. To try and commit to memory how the mountains fill my eyes, and not think too hard about why they confuse me.

To understand how such an underworld place can reach so high up.

Did He Exist?

One morning I was lying beneath a tree examining this foreign sky, to see if I could discern any difference between it and the sky I am so familiar with in London, when a man came up, with goats. I heard their bells and sat up. The man was whistling and looked at me. I looked back at him. He had a face like polished wood. His age was impossible to guess. The goats leapt about him, but he seemed oblivious to their antics.

I smiled at him and he smiled back and touched his cap. I touched mine in return before realising my head was bare. The goatherd laughed and I laughed back, and then he went on his way.

I could not speak to him, but nonetheless we communicated clearly.

I lay down and slept without dreams for the afternoon. When I awoke, I was deeply rested.

Small Things

Although smaller, there are things here that are more complex and heart-rending than mountains, despite their inferior visibility. I will learn to look hard at them, these objects that litter the world and so easily become states of mind. For example: the sun tugs the wildflowers skyward, where their petals wither. Birds are playful and busy. Women beat dusty mattresses and sing songs that sound like the movement of little rivers over rocks. Farmers smoke carved pipes and blow their smoke long and hard above their heads as they converse with each other. They pronounce their words with such measure and concentration, it is difficult to believe they are talking simply about cows or cheese or the weather, the subjects I imagine Alpine farmers talk about. I have never seen grown men enjoy a glass of milk more. Clean white sheets blow in the wind. Young girls wear their hair in buttery plaits and dress in bright colours, which they cover with pinafores. Their lips are often glossy. I glimpse their smooth plump calf muscles when they run. I am convinced their skin is soapy. It must be. It is soft at the edges, like something seen through water.

The bread here is shaped like mushrooms and is as heavy as rock. It fills me, scours me, cleans me. We eat it thick with cheese and sour jam for breakfast. I carry it inside me for hours like the presence of a friend. Shutters fling back to reveal checked curtains which are always about to billow. The air trembles occasionally with the drifting sounds of cowbells. The boys glance away when I say hello. They wear small gold earrings and have legs built for leaping. I have never seen such aggressive agility. They do not speak to the girls, who are also proud but, I feel, feign their shyness. They realise that I notice their eyes sparkle as they watch me eat my meals. They do not sparkle quite so hard at Sir Thomas. When I sparkle back, however, they look away. Like most girls, they do not know what it is they are looking at, what it is they are looking for. That, I suppose, is because they have never been told. They do not know the names of the things they need in their hearts, and in their bodies.

What Sir Thomas Loves

Sir Thomas loves this place, and simply to walk up a hill and sit on a bench and order something refreshing fills him with a feeling akin to ecstasy.

We sit outside an inn, and he pulsates with sheer joy at the raising of a tankard to his lips. I am touched, for once, by his hunger for living and burst out laughing, because at this moment in time our travels are suddenly filled with a sense of achievement.

Sir Thomas, I say, we have already travelled so far, and still have so far to go, and he laughs out loud as well, and puts his ale down on the table and looks at me.

Is this what you expected, Richard? Is there anything better on earth than this?

No, Sir Thomas, I doubt there is. I will drink to that, and so I lift my glass and he lifts his and we crash them together.

To travel, Richard!

Sir Thomas, to travel.

And Richard, to art! To the knowledge you will take back to London and transform the world of painting!

I toast this one in a manner that is a little more subdued. Oh, that I could do such a toast justice.

To art, Sir Richard. And to knowledge. To the things you love.

Ah, Richard.

His eyes fill with happy tears.

Another crash of metal, the slopping of liquid.

The foam of the beer as he drinks sticks to his moustache, and transforms him, for a moment, into an old man I do not know.

Families

Families here group together around the mountain like litters of puppies suckle a sweet, fat bitch. They know where they were born, and they know where they will be buried.

Families marry other families, and so this community becomes, truly, one big family linked by flesh that weaves its way around the village like a vine made from skin.

I imagine these families embracing the hills and mountains and giving birth to clouds and never speaking a word of it.

If you were happy to be embraced by these families, they would feed you well and nothing would be better than such closeness. Yet if you disagreed with them, to live here would be like being imprisoned by overwhelming flowers, the petals of which would make your hands bleed as you tore at them.

There must be families here who live in the mud and filth, but they are hidden from the Traveller. There are moments, however, when I am sure I can hear them mutter.

Nonetheless, it has occurred to me that I would like Maria to live for a while in the sunlight and air of such a place. Such solid parameters could only do her shaky ones good. I think of her next to these girls and imagine how wan she would appear. I would like to see Maria run panting up a hill. I would even like to see her kissed, briefly, by a strong brown boy, if only it would make her smile. I will write to Maria and attempt to make her laugh. I had not realised how simple her problems really are. Perhaps some sun might bleach her darkness blond. Some laughter will fill her with light.

Fathers and Sons

Everything is ordered here, and everything appears placid, except for the crucifix on my bedroom wall. The artist of this object has insisted I be made aware of every detail of Christ's torture, and how he suffered in a very human way for his otherworldliness. His eyes are twisted upwards, full of the knowledge that his father let this happen. His broken body, denied its natural collapse towards the earth, writhes in suffocation. Nails skewer and torment his splintered flesh and bones. His ribs leave no room for his breath to escape. His throat is full of congealed life. It is a terrible, moving image to have above one's bed, to sleep beneath, to wake beneath. When I wake I turn my eyes heavenward and see the souls of Christ's feet, bleeding, above me.

What kind of a Father was God to let his son suffer so?

Why did he not protect His only son?

What result could be worth such a sacrifice?

If God were mortal he would never have let anyone push nails through his own skin.

What then gave him licence to let it happen to his son?

The thought of it fills me with fury.

He is God. When I look at the world, I know he is the greatest artist, and, as such, was possessed of a terrible imagination. If he had wanted to, he surely could have invented a better way to communicate his message. We will stay here a while. Sir Thomas wants us to climb more mountains. He says again and again how much he enjoys the ale.

Climbing

We pull ourselves high and breathe the air hard.

There is little time for drawing, which does not worry me as perhaps it might elsewhere. I have realised this is not a place that lends itself easily to lines. Gradations of colour and tone stretch far beyond any line a person could draw, even in their heads, where the possibility of drawing is always infinite. My head is so fit to bursting with images, it seems almost unnecessary to apply them to paper. They are so vivid in front of me. Soon, however, I know I must or my hands might suffocate each other from boredom.

(Something preoccupying me: where does an image go if it is not drawn?)

A thought has wriggled its way into my mind and will not rest or resolve itself. It is this: if the mountain is in itself a perfect creation, why should I bother to recreate it, in a manner that cannot help but be inferior to the original?

This is a thought capable of dangerous seduction. It stumbles me in the dark recesses of my mind, fills me with lassitude then picks me up and continues: what, it whispers, in your field of vision, exists that only you could make?

I will mull on this problem. I will not let it take me over.

I reassure myself: a drawing is simply another type of mountain to scale. Another valley to explore.

The colours are predominantly cold or brown in this country, but they are colours that are occasionally lent some warmth when they bleed.

The green here is not to be trusted.

Blue lends itself to variations on the theme of blue. This blue stretches high and fades away, into clouds, wet like a watercolour with too much water. Like the hand of a heavy-handed artist has been at it.

Up in the sky, on the top of the mountains, we look down and the villages radiate like inconsequential ships. Clouds touch my face. Such hungry vertigo feeds my imagination. I draw a line with my finger in a pocket. And another. Sir Thomas holds his bony, thinning head up and laughs. He cracks his walking stick against the hard, high earth and slaps his thigh with his large spare hand. I don't doubt he would plant a flag if he had one. He laughs from deep inside himself. The sound of his laughter wraps around my throat and stops my eyes and stills my fingers as surely as a cork in a bottle stops the spilling of liquid. I can hear Maria's description: a sustained *cackleato*. She would linger on the words, then smile her laughter loud at me over the heads of others who cannot see her as clearly as I.

Sir Thomas puffs and groans and grins and swells at his victory over gravity.

He has climbed a hill!

Almost twice your age, Richard, he shouts as if I were on another peak. In my head my voice is dry and commanding: I am but a foot away, Sir Thomas, a foot.

I veil my wince and look up and feel the air on my skin. Permission granted to breathe again. I feel my legs. My hands touch the air that has fallen off my face. It is good to have such aching muscles. Muscles are, I have discovered, a distraction. I have not walked this far, or so high, ever. I have begun to make acquaintance with my limbs and lungs. They are more connected to each other than I ever knew. My blood must surely be bubbling now with all the air I have allowed it to drink. My belly presses hard against my innards. My back is full of spine, an arrow to my head.

I bite the air, the air bites me back.

I am almost happy.

We climb down and feel faint and proud but too tired to talk or boast. We retreat to our respective rooms, and scrub the mountain flush from our cheeks, perform our ablutions. I hear Sir Thomas sing through the wall, a line from a popular operetta. His German is clumsy and his voice booms and trembles. I smile at his pleasure. The peace in my room is tangible. Lie back awhile empty and clean and contemplate the ceiling, the blessed, silent relief of my dear companion, the ceiling.

A knock.

Richard, he calls, Richard. Ready for a small pre-supper refreshment yet boy?

Bid farewell to the ceiling.

Drinking

The tavern is as knotty and as dark as the inside of a tree.

Sir Thomas calls me fellow conqueror and cracks his tankard against mine.

We sing songs together, I make up the words, we laugh, he links his arm in mine and we sway on a worn, wooden bench, grinning at fellow revellers, other travellers, artistic types I strain to distance myself from. Please Lord, I pray into my beer, do not speak to me of pictures.

How marvellous, Sir Thomas bellows, and blows the froth from his ale into the air.

Oils? Delivered with a roar.

A fresh young face turns to him, looks at me, looks away, and turns back. Yes, oils, at home, but here, of course, I use only watercolour and pencil. I do not hear anymore, his voice is drowned in smoke and song and anyway, I do not want to hear it.

A thousand eyes, a million ears. We are close in intoxication and in the blurring of vision, if not in language or outlook.

My hands are rough things, clumsy, strong, unfamiliar appendages on the ends of my arms, transformed here to accommodate rocks and tankards and holding stout sticks. Not a brush in sight.

But what of my fingers, and the blood that connects them to my head?

Nights in a German Inn

We sleep in rooms of wood and lace beneath fat crisp sheets, stuffed with the plumage of a thousand slaughtered birds.

I can hear Sir Thomas split the night with his snoring in the room next to me. He makes the wall between us vibrate with his exertions. I cannot sleep, and so I watch what happens around me when the world thinks me unconscious. My arms are heavy and pin me to myself, my legs as still as old logs.

I feel the slyness beneath my lids, how my eyes might look closed to one who didn't know how to look.

This is what I see.

A small soft feather escapes and drifts away, a white thread curls in the cold night breeze. The miniature feet of tiny German mice whisper and tip toe around me.

(Every living thing born.)

The wood floor creaks. The suggestion of trees against the far wall, undeceived by my heavy lids, waving and bowing like old friends. The night moans gently. I smother my happiness with my pillow. (How was it I was born? Out of what coincidence or calamity? From what confluence of spirit and lust? My father's? My mother's? It is unthinkable. They lived clothed, even alone, I am convinced of it.)

I hear my father's voice. He whispers to me, so my sisters cannot hear, Richard, are you drunk?

He smiles beneath the sentence.

Father, I reply, I blush, I am simply myself.

I do not know what I mean.

The room moves slightly, as if it is afloat. It is not me, it is the walls.

They sway and laugh at the floor.

My father created me. Surely he would understand. I send him a thought, which I am convinced he will receive and reply to, when the wind's soft lips kiss mine as it creeps through the window and lies beside me.

I forget my father, and leap between tenses.

Time throws me to the wind and she adroitly catches me.

I murmur to her tell me a story. She replies at once, with wonderful clarity:

Oh! I have come a long way to reach you. From rocks. From stars. From the mouths of long-dead gods.

My night room is filled with such an amiable crowd! A sleepy excitement fills my heart and mind, to be honoured by such company.

The wind draws breath and begins. She tells me so many tales, my eyes nod with the strain of hearing her whisper, but I cannot fall asleep with such words in my ears. If only I could embrace such a storyteller.

I am filled with loneliness.

The wind tells me how she wraps her thin arms around the hats of young girls and lifts them off their heads and flings them into rivers. She tells me how she has blown a jewel into the path of a beggar, a bullet into the heart of a banker. She has tickled the cheeks of babies, dashed ships against rocks and then, consumed with remorse, pulled survivors ashore by their coat tails and petticoats. She has fanned fires, destroyed towns and then comforted the cheeks of fire fighters with a breeze. She has boiled water for the tea of explorers, melted ice caps, irritated old women damp with rain, blown curtains open to reveal illicit kisses, pushed back the petals of flowers to show a child a dancing fairy, cooled the brow of the Prince of Denmark when he was a child. Her stories jostle for space in my mind until I beg her to stop. I can only hear so many tales in one night. She leaves me, lamenting my exhaustion, and tells me, sighing. She is lonely again.

I keep the window open, to hear more clearly the movement of birds. There is an owl out there. It, too, is alone. It sings like a foghorn.

A strange bird to hear here, it sings the same song it did in Chatham, but is, without doubt, a different bird. I suspect its wings are browner and touched with a trembling hint of red. I would laugh if they were. Imagine, nature applied so accurately to geography!

Do birds adapt their plumage to the place in which they are born?

How would a bird choose a colour for its feathers in London?

No wonder the pigeons in Trafalgar Square are so dull.

Wood in Germany

There are so many things growing here, things you cannot see, you would doubt the possibility of cold, but despite the warmth that fills the air it is a cold place.

This food must have fought hard to be born, to push through such earth, that it must surely remain cold even as the sun shines hot on its surface.

For this, I have realised, is a frigid country, even in summer. There is grass, of course, green grass that covers the brown earth, but I do not believe in it enough to credit it with real colour or any warmth.

As a matter of fact, it has occurred to me that the grass here is full of deceit, too pretty, too full of spring to be real. Its green is too consistent, too constantly applied.

It is like rouge on an old cheek.

I could never lie on this thick, soft grass.

There is an undercurrent of secrecy, of violence in the genial faces of our hosts. It is best to be alert. Of course, their language is not necessarily secretive. Perhaps it is only my lack of knowledge of the words they use. But their sunburnt hands are as sly as they are strong. It is wise to be aware of the places they could go. Of the things they might touch without permission.

As our landlord speaks to us of breakfast options, his fingers drum the leather of his trousers. His face and his hands tell me different things, as they move in different directions.

I prefer bodies unified in their messages.

Our plates are obscene and nourishing. Grinning sausages, shiny potatoes, beer. Eggs with yolks like orbs. Milk that coats my tongue and makes me cough. Cheese it takes a strong wrist to slice.

However, notwithstanding my reservations about the honesty of this place, I must admit I have never so deeply enjoyed the sensation of swallowing, or the feeling of a full, tight belly. I am all body and appetite, and arrive at the table like another might arrive for a fight he secretly craves.

I have a picture in me of all this, but cannot place it, cannot put a colour to it, nor a line, nor a true word.

It is to do with a sensation that sets my bones shivering and my mind racing in a direction I find hard to follow. It is to do with wood and spirits, which are more evident here than at home. On the wall of the breakfast room, faces come at me from wood knots. Small, leering faces, with slurred shoulders and peaked caps and gnarled fingers. It is difficult not to imagine how their limbs might swell beneath their undergarments, quite despite the fact that the image of them, their carved images, stop where their shoulders begin.

I have been forced to sit and chew with my face averted from their fixed, over-spirited, impish stares.

Children roar and laugh at their repellent features, but I would warn them of their seriousness, if their mamas weren't so close and protective, their fathers so brimful of misguided confidence in an art that might pretend to be cheerful, but is, in reality, an accurate rendering of possibility.

I shake Sir Thomas off me and walk in the woods alone, to try and imagine the man who carved such compelling aberrations. There is a very present feeling of metamorphosis in these German trees, a metamorphosis that is transferred into the carvings the artists mould from their limbs. Of speechless creatures coming from wood, curling out from under the dormant flowers, from beneath the wings of flying things.

Where are the fairies here? Are they as busy as they are at home?

Perhaps it was not an artist who built such sculptures.

The thought starts me shivering.

He first hit me in the forest, when I could hardly walk I was so little.

I had seen a cat, a large, dark cat and told him so, and he told me there were no cats in this forest, and I said no, he was not right. And he hit me. He was not much older than me, but I can still feel his fist on my face, whenever I walk beneath trees. He called himself my friend. Then the memory fades, and once again, the branches become somewhere to hide. I trust the watchful birds to keep guard, as the small animals burrow more deeply into the earth, for safety.

Sir Thomas has laughed at me for what he calls my fancy in seeing anything in these wooden figurines.

They are simply toys, Richard, carved from dead stories. Ah, boy, wait till we get to Italy.

A smirk, followed by dismissal. These stories are alive in me, and in the people here, and they almost shout out to be heard. Sir Thomas cannot hear such things. He blocks himself from them. He may travel extensively, but travelling for him is simply a reiteration of what he thinks he already knows. He travels to see his prejudices carved in stone. But he is easy to block. I look away and he is not there. I do not doubt for a second that there is something in these shapes beyond the delineation of the carver's tool and eye. A story gluts each blade of grass in this strange country, stories we are not privy to, not having been born here. These stories come from somewhere true. Why, otherwise, would they be born in someone's mind? Who put them there? Images are bled from me in tiredness.

Drinking songs drift up through the floorboards and lull me to sleep.

Guilt

Sir Thomas is so good and healthy after his climbing that I am filled with guilt at my churlishness at his pleasure. I must give him his due, his lack of complication is not always an irritation. Sometimes, it is rare, but just sometimes his jolly face and manner are a tonic to my head, which lately has been as tired as my climbing limbs.

Without any intention on his part, he has let me glimpse the possibility of a more simple world.

I remember: walking to make pictures of the boats in Medway. The heavy way their shapes docked inside me, and how I struggled to extract them. How the water lapped beside my easel, and how its rhythm frustrated me in its possible combinations.

I know there is a confused logic to every thought I have. This is a clear, good, reassuring feeling because it tells me that every idea has a counter-idea, every fear some solace in its very human fallibility.

All that aside, I must say: Sir Thomas is in awe of the mountains in the same way another man might be in awe of his bank manager.

The Idea of Italy

Germany is a strange apprenticeship for Italy, which disturbs me in anticipation. Here it is not lines that are so apparent in nature but shapes and undercurrents. I cannot imagine the laying on of colour in such a place, but know some have done it well.

In Italy I predict a clear light, a mastery of line, a marriage of idea and colour, of spirit and intention, the transformation of rock into marble. But I do not wish to wish too much.

The Rhine is the brown wash across an old painting. I feel we will need to travel south to strip it clean from the images it obscures.

I have dreamt and shivered the paintings I expect to see. I have seen them in my mind's eye, I think, and yet not believed them. But perhaps my mind is wrong. How could it possibly anticipate pictures I have not seen? Perhaps my anticipation is to do with a kind of self-gratification I need to see the images that will confirm the correctness of my path. Perhaps my prejudices are as firmly cemented as Sir Thomas'.

We stride along narrow streets, my travelling companion and I. It is inevitable, perhaps, that sometimes we do not notice the windows that we pass.

Sir Thomas delights in my trepidation and is smug in the knowledge of his previous visits. He has seen these images and speaks of them with propriety, as if he invented them himself.

If his face could rub itself together in glee it would. His stout little nose curls up to his eyes, which squint at me with a knowing geniality. He has seen them before, he tells me again and again and again. He knows what is to come, but I would prefer not to listen to his preview. The words he employs when he speaks of pictures are all wrong. His is a mind filled with images that stack together like the dry leaves of a ledger.

I admit he is a kind and generous and harmless man, but that does not mean he is not wrong.

The intimations are too clear to ignore. In truth, Sir Thomas would shout with as much joy at the sight of cool pale ale as he would at a correct line, the perfect intimation of another's experience.

(But then perhaps he is right in this. His is a life certainly filled with more light-heartedness than mine. His enjoyment of the world makes me thin and tight with jealousy.)

At moments, I believe he forgets himself and cannot see who I am.

Different Architects

Italy. The word has become associated in my mind with another arrival. Another room, another ceiling, another sky. Different architects, different sounds from different mouths. I am filled with awe at the infinite permutations of travel. The infinite combinations. The infinite reworkings of a well trod path.

Strange to think of the horses pulling the carriage the same way every day, and each day smelling and seeing something different.

I would like, I think, to converse with the horses, to ask them about what they have seen, how the cold, hard bit feels between their teeth, the difference between pulling a man and a girl. I would ask them if they do their job gladly, or if they long to be a different beast, a milking cow perhaps, a lap dog, or a kitten. I would ask them if they ever plot revolution, or smell the different grasses as they canter down a rocky hill.

I am curious as to whether they miss their mothers and in what way the men who drive them so hard differ in cruelty and intent. If they ever bolted or are whipped hard. If they long to read or to look at pictures.

I share another carriage with Sir Thomas. We have already been in so many together.

I never spent so long in such proximity to another human being.

We know more about each other now than we did before. For example: we know to ignore each other's moans, which increase without our permission, when the journey becomes interminable. We know how to remain silent for long stretches.

This has become our modest, if shared talent.

We also now know that we do not share the same vocabulary.

Another Arrival

We leave Switzerland behind us. We pass through the border, which is filled with young men, loitering in uniform.

A sense of unrest is present in the glances soldiers direct at us.

We make it clear to anyone who will listen that we are not French, but English, the defeators of Napoleon. We gave them back their country, Sir Thomas repeatedly informs me, but it has once again become, it would seem, many countries. Fighting is in the air.

The gradual stripping away of officialdom is like the countryside loosening its collar. With every village we pass through, the eyes of the inhabitants become more indolent, more charming. The girls look up into our carriage, their mouths parted slightly. It is rather unnerving. I look away, and look back again to see them once more.

Oh, despite its vulgarity, such a soft place!

The women have heated skin.

I am so immediately intoxicated that I do something I rarely do.

I speak my mind.

Sir Thomas and I are drinking in a small inn. We look at each other and smile, hearing the sounds of Italy around us.

It is a noisy place, but the voices are not speaking German, and so the atmosphere is noticeably different from anywhere we have come from. In Germany, voices sounded like chopping carrots, in Italy, like bubbling oil.

I drink and my head becomes immediately light.

Sir Thomas, I say, this may perhaps sound foolish, but I feel we have arrived in a place where everything seems to be in the process of both being born and dying.

Sir Thomas laughs as if I have said the funniest thing in the world. I think my seriousness makes him nervous.

Ah Richard. Surely the same could be said about London?

I think for a moment.

But in London, transitions are separate. A child is born. Someone dies.

Here, everything seems to be happening at once.

In the midst of Life, Richard, we are in death. Do not forget that.

Lord, the man tires me. He does not ask me what I mean. I ask myself, and realise I do not know.

So I change the subject and talk about the quality of wine. Sir Thomas breathes easily.

But, I cannot help but notice it everywhere, dead things surrounded by eyes and mouths brimming to overflow with life. Italy is a place of tumultuous noises and yielding colours, of gazes that slip and hold.

There is a feeling here not of deceit, but of concealment: in the copious skirts of women, in the deep pockets of young boys, in the eyes of everyone. I can imagine a hand moving smoothly into mine and grabbing it so tightly it would still the veins in my wrist.

Everything is soft that breathes here, and everything brutal is hidden in every soft breath. Lakes fell from the mountains we came from. Like the descent into laughter from the sermon of sedate Switzerland, a place of measurement and excellent ale, of churches empty of images. Churches full of a quiet, good faith, but no eye.

Italy. The joyfulness that touches every sound in every alley, even in the sound of a weeping child.

A pot clangs, a donkey glares at me with a sardonic eye.

Hands fly up to argue, the eyes merry, theatrically tragic.

Every gesture a song.

Mothers and Fathers and Children

In Chatham I grew up to the sound of hammers.

I recall slipping into the great sheds where the mighty men of war were built, to draw their interlocking lines and masts, or running, beneath a wet sheet of a sky, to the cornfields or orchards or hop fields with my watercolours. I hid damp and cold, and looked close at the shape and colour of bark or apple or blade of grass, and attempted to describe an ant from memory, or a pebble, or a clod of thick earth. I searched for nests and never disturbed an egg but wondered how best to render its shape, which begins nowhere and is never finished.

I hunted elusive light to escape the squalid streets that surrounded us. My father asked me again and again, Richard, where do you go?

I could not tell him. My images were powerful because they were invisible to everyone but myself.

My sisters, my brothers, my life chorus: Richard, where do you go?

My father loves to look at pictures. I could not show him mine when I was little. I was too ashamed of the lines that did not go where I wanted.

I have seen fathers here swell with pride at the sight of their ragged offspring doing nothing more impressive than eating. Such sights make me look away. A father's love is knotted in me tight, too tight to draw, whereas mothers are a space I do not know how to describe.

Italy is a country in which it is unimaginable not to have a mother.

If your mother is no longer alive, in every church, another mother with a gentle face and open arms can be found to kneel before.

I realise I am an aberration, a twice motherless man.

My mother died, to be replaced by another, who also died, and when I was little there were no mothers in any churches, only angry fathers and bleeding sons.

Perhaps in England mothers are weaker, or, perhaps, gentler, than fathers.

The sounds in the street are even louder than the hammers, but the noises are touched with exuberance. I envy these children. I envy their smooth, warm plumpness and their odd elegance, the smothering arms and wet kisses of their mothers. The urchins of Chatham would look like drowned kittens next to these young gods.

Perhaps my admiration for the way they look is the merely sentimental ramblings of a traveller. It must be true that they have their fair share of weeping behind closed doors, their fair share of beatings. Even so, no sentiment on my half alters the fact of the ubiquitous sunlight. These are children born into sun.

I no longer remember her face, although I know I carry it inside me.

Where is mother now, I asked my father.

Father was sitting, looking at a wall. He shook his head to my question.

I am your mother now, Richard, he replied.

I was shocked.

Father, you are not my mother.

In a swift, violent movement he smashed his fist onto the delicate table beside him. It cracked and buckled.

A maid came to the door and stood and looked and scratched her leg. Father ignored her, and slumped in his chair.

I will have to suffice.

I stood my ground.

If she is not here, she must be somewhere. Where then, Father, can I find her? If she is not here, where has she gone?

He sat again, his hand bleeding.

She is dead and gone to Heaven.

I cried then.

Well, I shall go there too and fetch her back. How do I get there?

You have to die, Richard, and then you might arrive, but only if you have been good. But you can never bring her back. People do not return from Heaven.

He continued to stare at the wall.

I did not move.

And was mama good?

Silence.

Yes, she was good.

He did not look at me, and I, suddenly, did not like looking at him.

And so I left. The maid touched my hair, but I did not know the touch of her hand and pushed it away.

I did not know where to go.

Religious Sense

Despite the abundance of churches and the opulent crucifixes that adorn the necks of every female, there is surprisingly little religious sense here. Although priests abound, their faces do not indicate great self-denial. The women pray with hands that would just as happily cook or stroke. They would swap this God for another without a thought, like a vegetable exchanged for a fresher one, in a corrupt market.

The devil, I can almost hear them mutter, what would the devil matter, if he made our lives more pleasant? After all, he too was once an angel, like we are.

It is enough to know he was once good.

I enter a church and see the worshippers stained by the reflection of the glass windows. At first the sight is beautiful, but the closer I look, the more it becomes apparent that the rainbow light lends their skin the appearance of violent bruises. They look touched, damaged, wrong.

I would not like to suggest that God was making something apparent to me, but must admit, it did occur to me. Why would people look so damaged in a church if God had not willed me to see it? Why, unless they were meant to be punished?

It is all very beautiful and very worrying.

Venice

Venice could not have been designed by a mortal. I would not believe it even if an angel were to inform me it were so, and showed me the paperwork to prove it. Even the beggars are perfect, with their soulful eyes and elongated, supplicating hands. The lower classes of people are far more picturesque than anywhere else I have been: their grace of motion and noble carriage are striking. I have tried to make pictures of their likenesses and in doing so compared them to my mental images of their equivalents in London. The comparison is nothing short of ludicrous. They are so far removed from the sickly pallor and whining gestures of the English poor as to be from another planet. Perhaps in England, having had only one God, we never had enough God to go around. Here they have had such a plethora of gods, and these gods, if we are to believe our Ovid, were so easy with their affections, it is no wonder the mortal population inherited something of their beauty. Gods and their blood must have somehow filtered through to the populous, but whatever the reason or cause, it is difficult to imagine where else such lowly people might have found such aristocratic bearing. Perhaps from the swans and trees the gods became to couple with women, perhaps from the delicate clouds they hid in.

I have heard that Lord Byron used to swim in the canal and can only assume his submersion was a form of baptism, an homage, an act of devotion. If I were to allow my head beneath the waters of Venice, I would not breathe again, happy to welcome such sweet suffocation. I have walked the narrow lanes at dawn and seen buildings emerge, newborn into the light, built of cobweb, steam and precious jewels.

I have floated alone down the Grand Canal at midnight, convinced that such palazzos are, despite their bricks and mortar, edifices built from dreams. I have seen the pigeons explode at sunset above St Marks, the cacophony of their wings like applause at such magnificence. It must be one of the most gorgeous temples conceivable. No material has been spared. The range of the most costly and various marbles and mosaics is astonishing. The altars are the richest I have ever seen, adorned to excess and with the lights burning in various degrees of intensity, the incantations of the most sombre and otherworldly priests imaginable officiating and children, old men and women, young, veiled beautiful women, in fact, all manner of people kneeling and unified throughout this fantastic interior, an extraordinary sight for the eye.

Venice is a city built of pictures that have floated into my head like a lobster into a pot. I will die with them in my heart, and be joyful at the heat they generate, at the impossibility of them ever escaping my mind.

But the gondoliers and the street sellers! They must be God's joke on a people who have allowed themselves to become indifferent to the beauty that surrounds them. They are the greatest villains on earth, or, to be entirely accurate, water. Sir Thomas and I were conveyed by two who swore and shouted at each other and, after a few minutes of this violent confrontation actually struck one another with their broad oars, yet still, on delivering us, asked for a gratuity! Everyone here who has something to sell seems to take for granted their right to plunder travellers. They expect to be paid for the slightest services, for example, telling one the time, or pointing the way to the market, or even smiling. I am surprised it hasn't caught on, and half expect Sir Thomas to demand a few coins when I pass him the salt at supper. When we leave our hotel they swarm about us with cruel, greedy faces and clutching fingers, anxious, like their own detestable fleas and mosquitoes, to get the last drop out of you. Never have I been made so aware of the difference between men. They look upon us as if we were wildly and extravagantly rich. I am the first to acknowledge, we perhaps are by their standards. But I violently object to their assumptions. I object to anybody assuming anything about me. There have been moments when I have exploded with a rage that has surprised even me.

Sir Thomas, ever the experienced traveller, patronises me with sniggers, murmuring beneath his breath, Ah! Richard, you will learn, you will learn.

At times I could have gladly exchanged him for the worst of them. But their architecture and their paintings are enough to assuage the wrath of even a misjudged and ignorant artist.

Italian Painting

I almost could not look, because looking drained everything from me, and replaced it with a void I had never before recognised in myself. Jealousy.

Where did they get it from, this blazing perfection? And how did so many receive the gift?

I have attempted to convey this idea in letters home, to friends, to my family. My words, however, are such thin things. They could not move or inspire the reader as much as a toenail painted by Tintoretto. I have had to depend on words that reflect nothing of the experience of looking, and so feeling.

However, if I am to be bled dry I will be grateful for my lack of every drop.

Tintoretto. The Miracle of St Mark. The fury of the painter only matched by the consummate fury of the subject. The trembling, raging goodness of such paint. It is terrible and fascinating that a man could summon such images. Or Veronese, full of daylight. The artist manipulating the material until the material itself disappears. The soft, rabid paint of Titian. The Italian mouth of the Bellini Madonna, in a few strokes annihilating all of our preconceptions about the spiritual laziness of these people.

I walk with my arm around the shoulders of Giorgione's ghost, which is restless with the impotence of unfinished pictures and premature death. I would like to protect his spirit as it walks the alleyways of Venice, haunted by Titian, who is trying to kill him, whose wild breath I have felt upon my cheek, his rage undimmed by extinction. Giorgione trembles, filled with the terrible knowledge that lightening would strike him many times.

Giorgione did not know how to protect himself.

He was not mad, and he was pursued. He knew this much and was not believed.

Poor Giorgione, in danger of his life, painting pictures which dissolve into the deflected light of the canals. Painting pictures that dull-witted people find impossible to fathom because they are not full of the meanings most people crave. These men who stand perplexed before Giorgione must have dull safe marriages and reveal nothing to their wives, because there is nothing for them to reveal. The few women I have witnessed looking at his paintings appear somewhat more confused than the men. They glance, turn away, then turn back again and look with wide eyes. Perhaps women expect less and so see more. I do not know. These paintings turn everything around that can be turned around.

Paintings to fall into.

Sir Thomas reads aloud from Vasari in front of each painting until I crumble in embarrassment. He finds people to dine with us. I think he has begun to find my silences dull.

I do not blame him. I am mute to him.

I cannot speak about painting to Sir Thomas. After all, I could not speak German to Germans because I do not speak their language. Somehow, although our language anchors us to our geographical origins, in the space that truly counts, we bear no relation to each other, are not kinsmen. We come from different places on this planet. From cities so far, far away from each other, the possibility of communication between us is impossible.

I am nothing and so must begin again.

Ballad Mongers

When I was a child, Ballad Mongers visited our town to sell their songs. They hung their pages up for inspection like lines of sheets on washing day.

People peered into them and as they read, imagined the sound they might make when sung.

I recalled these itinerants when I received word from my father.

I held the pages of his letter before me and could have sworn I heard music.

The weight and texture of the paper of my father's letter were as familiar to me as his face. The shape of his writing echoed the strong shape of his good hands.

To hold his words was at once immensely familiar and immensely strange. Like seeing someone you did not expect to see in a place you have never visited before.

He wrote to me of my brothers and sisters (well), and of his business bronzing and water gilding (steady). He described paintings he had recently seen (nothing interesting) and briefly discussed the weather (bad) and friends (friendly). In other words, he wrote me an entirely predictable letter.

I carry it in my pocket like an anchor.

Letters Home

Sir Thomas is buried too deeply inside that corpulent body of his and will not read the signs that surround him. But he writes all the time, despatching letters to his family, so many and such long letters that surely they must include the number of ants we have seen and weigh the amount of sunlight every day that touches his sturdy shoulders.

I am sure I caught him counting the crumbs on the table after supper.

A cigar, Richard?

I accept one and look for his notebook. Surely this momentous event must be recorded. Richard has smoked a cigar!

What does he not leave out though? He writes of everything but the hard, true things, the ones that permeate our conversation without a word spoken.

I have begun to read some of his letters. I am ashamed to admit it, but was too filled with curiosity to resist.

The first time, he left his letter on the sideboard and went to fetch a book. I heard him conversing with our landlady. I picked up his letter and read it. I did not realise we had done so much.

Oh, how he goes on! About what we have eaten, what we have seen.

His letters are contracted like a housekeeper might order her weekly accounts in pages and pages of lists. I would not be surprised if he drafted his letters in columns and has a formula for every feeling.

He writes like a genial accountant.

I am filled with frustration at the thought of the conversations we could have had, the letters he might write home. I know that this is unfair of me, but in truth, I cannot veil my thoughts. I dwell, almost obsessively I must admit, on the exchanges we might have had if he had been someone else. I feel an overwhelming need to have my assumptions challenged.

Namely: a dissection, a clarification of what happens in the space that occurs between the mind and the image. We could have discussed why images are necessary. We might have argued deep into the night about the possible existence of a world more real than the one we now inhabit, or disagreed about the meandering degree of truth-telling that exists at the heart of all truths. We might have analysed the complicated urges that make a man want to own an image when he has seen the thing he wants to draw, which is in effect the thing that moves him most, either in passion, in curiosity or in the spirit of experimentation. Sir Thomas, I would like to ask you: in your opinion, which is bigger, mountains or grass? A drop of rain, a sliver of glass? The potential of a calf or a lamb? The power of the sun or moon? Mars or Venus? Woman or man? Sir Thomas, tell me, what is the difference between a song and a picture in its recreation of a feeling? Sir Thomas, why are some sculptures considered great and others indifferent? Would you really be able to see the difference, Sir Thomas?

And, Sir Thomas, tell me, what is it that separates me from you.

I would dearly like to know.

He speaks to me about the origins of architecture, but not about the bricks and the slaves and the heat and the flies, or the desire of one man to own more bricks than his neighbour.

I have discovered I do not want to know about the bricks so much as to understand the impulse that said to someone, somewhere, I am tired of retreating inside myself and so must build a wall.

Yes. I would like to learn more about the origins of rooms.

Sir Thomas, tell me how a flower speaks and how I might better read the words that fill the sky. Sir Thomas, can you translate a bird's song? Would you like to try?

We could start with a common trill.

Sir Thomas, tell me, now, about the space between you and I and what fills it. Tell me why a story should be transformed into an image.

Tell me how the image might transmit both an atmosphere of the real and a semblance of imitation, which, in its constant ambiguity, ensures the life of the subject so depicted.

Every line is full of lies and every lie is full of truth.

The problem exists in the sorting, the sieving, the ruthless looking. But you cannot teach a man such things. He has to find them out himself. That is my travelling sorrow. I am impatient. These are only some of the questions and some of the observations that never gain entrance into Sir Thomas' missives home.

Maria Writes

A slim letter and stained, from grubby fingers and perhaps tears.

I wish, unfairly perhaps, that she would not tell me the things she tells me. Because once I have her words inside my head they stick and will not budge.

She tells me, in abrupt, painful sentences, of how she sews and yawns and that she cannot sleep for dreaming too hard. She writes, quite simply, of her love of the colour blue, and how she will dress in no other and of how she has decided not to speak for a week or eat more than four mouthfuls of food a day, and how she has abstained from kissing the cheeks of loved ones, in order to know their minds more closely, and refrained from smelling flowers, so she will learn to look more closely at their shapes.

She tells me father is too busy to notice anything and her brothers never speak to her.

She enquires about my travels with questions that are close enough to my own way of thinking to make me uneasy: Come home, Richard, and tell me about the different light. Have you held your face to the stars?

She tells me she cannot imagine what we eat.

She is mute about Sir Thomas.

She tells me little about my family, although I can imagine what they are doing. But they do not know the places I move through. That is the difference.

It Is Difficult to Believe It Exists

We travel to Rome through dusted golden countryside.

We drink wine in our carriage to alleviate the discomfort. Sir Thomas becomes voluble.

One field appears, full of poppies, then another overflowing with yellow flowers.

There are no birds in the sky.

The coachman breaks into a mournful song.

My senses cannot take much more.

Sir Thomas sighs and sips.

I love this country, Richard. Do you feel that?

That you love it, Sir Thomas, or that I love it?

Both. I am a different man here, Richard. Something in Italy casts England away from me.

I look at him. Apart from his cheeks, which are red from the sun, he looks exactly like the man I left England with.

I am curious.

What is it that has been cast from you, Sir Thomas?

A reticence, perhaps, to speak one's mind honestly. A reserve in one's attitude to strangers. I feel more forthcoming. Do you know what it is I am speaking of?

I think for a moment.

I think of the women I have seen here whom I would like to embrace. The thought has occurred to me more often in Italy than in any other time of my life.

I have blushed more in a week in the streets of Venice than I have in a year in London.

I think of the unspeakable paintings.

These are thoughts I find impossible to communicate. And so I lie. Yes, I think I do understand. It is in the air. The air and the light. It is more accommodating than at home.

Accommodating, Richard? Of what?

Sometimes you speak the truth despite yourself.

I am caught out.

Accommodating of pleasure, Sir Thomas. When such air touches the skin, it creates benevolence in one's attitude towards one's fellow man. Silence. He thinks. Then turns to me.

Do you know, Richard, I do think I agree with what you are saying.

He turns his head and gazes intently at something in the far distance. Look at that, Richard. It is hard to believe it exists.

I look towards where he is pointing. A tower on a hill, its edges dissolving in the sunlight, its base hovering above the earth. Tall cypress trees flank it like ladies-in-waiting. A thin road curves up to it. The whole scene is absent of people.

Sir Richard is right. It is difficult to believe that it exists.

A Dream in Rome

I dreamt there was too much lethargy in Rome.

I dreamt that this lethargy was endemic and that the only way it could be eradicated would be to frighten people here into understanding that their own energy, their own possibility for transformation, like the sky in a Tintoretto or the discovery of the edge in a Titian, was by the spilling of blood. That sometimes transformation demands, nay, deserves, blood. Their religion is wrong. It is wrong because it satiates their need for the body, which it gives them at every ceremony and makes them self-satisfied. Their capacity for painting has disappeared from them. There are reasons for this. The church and the painting are inextricably connected, and cannot, should not be separated here, but the laziness of these people has forced a weakness to occur in the connection. They have a greater need for moral strictness than anywhere else I have been, but they have diffused their religion with sensuality. I am overwhelmed by the people I see in the street. They rub their crucifixes and spit. The men and boys walk into churches looking at the girls.

I have seen them feign prayer and slip a hand beneath the skirts of kneeling supplicants. Seeing such believers is like seeing a river stripped of light, a woman without breasts, the sky without a sun, a Bellini without a Madonna, yet this should be unimaginable, for never was a country so blessed with the possibility of beatitude. But no one has woken them up.

In my dream I slit the throat of their lazy Pope and replace him with a blazing Angel. When I wake from this dream, I know that it is not wrong, but that this country, emotionally and spiritually, is wrongly located. Sir Thomas calls it a charming place and is worn out from winking. It is as charming as a deconsecrated church operating as a brothel and filled with the most beautiful whores imaginable. This dream has made me sad and nervy. I do not feel myself.

The Colosseum

After a month in Rome, I am glutted on ruins and see things in their cracks and crevices I never noticed before.

We visit the Colosseum, again. It is a different place every time.

Cats mewl and curl around our legs as we attempt to wander through the crumbs of this once terrible place. The crickets scream incessantly and the sun is white. The wind lifts the dust into our eyes. Beggars cry out at the gates, and filthy Gypsy children attempt to slip their fingers into our pockets. Sir Thomas stamps on the bare feet of a little girl, who runs away howling. Her cries bounce off the heartless stone.

I try to intervene, to protest.

Sir Thomas, she is only a child.

He rises before me, stout and indignant.

She is grown enough to know right and wrong. She was intent on robbing me, Richard. And then, where would we be?

My protest is lame, my words impotent.

But Sir Thomas, she is probably no better than a slave. A child slave. He does not dignify my observation with a response and walks away from me with an angry back.

This place fills me with sadness and dread. This is a place where Christians were killed, but our outrage at such crimes is, I feel, a little misplaced. I cannot wander through this ancient tomb and not think of our own terrible Tyburn, where men swung for crimes that, more often than not, should have warranted little more than a rebuke.

I read that the Emperor Hadrian gave the populace spices to honour his mother-in-law and ordered essence of balsam and saffron to be poured over the seats in the Colosseum. He considered them sweet smells to watch death by. The image plagues me.

But, perhaps it was not so simple and I should not dwell on a history that may have no basis in reality. Truths shift and alter with each telling. I could imagine how I might write another's story, or even, and this is the strangest thought, my own, and how, if held up against the life it was meant to replicate, this story would seem to appear riddled with holes and artifice. Nothing could reproduce my breath here or now. Who can tell the thoughts that crowded Hadrian's head as he sat by his loathed wife's mother and watched screaming men and women and even children have their limbs torn away. Who can tell?

History is more and more unclear to me. I do not know who to believe or which story to heed. It is easier to draw, to look at the curve of rock or stone or brick and to try and fathom how it interacts with the sky and the earth than it is to contemplate the mechanics of the mind of the man who ordered that this violent architecture be placed so perfectly.

Greece

Patras Argos Mycenae Corinth Athens ...

The sounds of these words! As dusty as the schoolroom, as difficult as memories I have dreamt but never experienced. It is hard to reconcile myself to the fact that these words are, quite simply, the names of towns, practical naming devices like Chatham or London or Hastings. But I cannot grasp it. They sound like words waiting to be translated, tainted with the blood of animal battles or fetid romances that have straddled time. Words that clang like a faint bell on the edge of my mind, calling together a congregation of nursery stories, of Ulysses, of Troy, of Helen, of giant fictitious horses and women who turn into fish, of songs that could kill a man, of gods and demigods and heroes.

The sounds of these words in no way prepare the weary traveller for the very real filth spilling out from every doorway. How different the reality to the actuality! History has crumbled these towns as effectively as if it had taken a sledgehammer to their bricks and statues and books. But the more they crumble, the more mythical, the more buried, their origins become. These are the elements of Greece about which our teachers remained mute, but perhaps their silence was born of ignorance. The stained marble, the crumbling fingertips of masterpieces, the filthy huts that coexist with tear-stained splendour. The ruins of the ancients have become as integral to the living habits of the locals as bread. But with less sustenance, less meaning. The people here live in such a strange way, they hardly feel like fellow humans, but yet their curiosity in me is mirrored by my own in them. Their eyes are almost uniformly beautiful, thick lashed, heavy and profoundly and deeply dark, but they hug their filth and dirty habits to them like friends.

Perhaps though, in such a country where the air tastes like a wonderful drink, they do not crave the same order as I do. Their lives are as dreamt as they are lived.

The air is full of lemons and wild thyme and the gentle percussion of goat bells. It tastes like syrup tinged with something harsh and insubstantial, perhaps the whispering of ghosts who stand on every corner and behind every bush. The sun cannot be the same sun we have in England. It might be perhaps a distant cousin, but nothing closer.

Greece is populated with characters from fairy tales, the diluted descendants of Gods.

I have seen a pirate with a knife in his boots speak in a language I cannot recognise, to a woman who leant up to lick his cheek as tenderly as a child.

I have seen an old woman walk through a village with a sheep leaping at her side linked to her hand by a piece of string. I have seen a child in a doorway, a goat asleep at her feet as she spun the narrow wool from its back.

I have tried to distract my restless mind by eating fresh tomatoes. I eat them like apples and they taste of the sun and the air.

I have watched a gypsy family sing a vicious, beautiful song. I have no access to those words, but I understood their sentiment with a fluency that surprised me.

I have heard incantations to ward off profanity and sinfulness. I have heard shepherds recite poetry beneath cypress trees. I have tasted oil squeezed from the small hard berries of the olive tree.

Everything Exists Only Once

In a market Sir Thomas calls to me Will you look at this, Richard.

Busy as I am examining pots, I am obedient to his summons.

He is examining a fossil at a stall. A long-dead insect curled into stone, permanently asleep.

It is worn out, plain and beautiful.

Do you like it, Richard?

I do, Sir Thomas. Very much. Do you?

It is terribly overpriced. But I have not seen one like it before.

Will you buy it, then?

He thinks, strokes it with a large finger, mops his brow.

No, Richard, I do not think I will. There will be others to buy, similar to this one, but less expensive, I am sure of it.

The fossil is the price of modest ale in London.

The seller begins to yell, no no no. You are wrong. None cheaper, none cheaper.

Sir Thomas hands him back his relic and we walk on, attempting to ignore the man's irate cries.

Sir Thomas puts on his moral face.

Perhaps I should have bought it, Richard. But I do not like to support these thieves.

Thieves, Sir Thomas?

Yes, Richard, thieves. He was a thief. It was obvious. His eyes.

I think about the fossil but do not tell Sir Thomas that he should have bought it.

He will never find another one like it.

Looking Becomes Lines

This is a seductive country. It facilitates desires to drowse in the afternoon and wake and eat and then wander the streets until the early morning. Its climate encourages nocturnal activities.

I have become drunk on retsina and sucked the harsh smoke of their cigarettes deeply and gratefully into my lungs.

I have felt the heat from kitchens cooking food I cannot name. I do not recognise their smells. They are mostly delicious and make me light-headed with hunger, even when I have recently eaten.

(Sir Thomas has begun to speak wistfully of Roast Dinners.)

I have tried to read the signs around me but cannot. This Greek script dances and leaps about the page. It blocks my passage to comprehension. It insists that this place and these people will continue to remain enigmatic to me. I am dependent on translation, which makes me feel somewhat detached, as if I were hearing and looking at the world through a thin muslin cloth.

I have seen Sir Thomas' face swell with the effort of bargaining for a carpet.

I have tried to make my watercolours echo with the sounds of the port.

I have painted endless windows, and the faces that look in and out of them.

I have attempted to draw connections between the air and the earth.

The blue doorways are wonderfully cheerful, and the villages look like polished white rocks that have been stained by the colour of the sky.

Greece is a luminous bone, an infinite and fascinating graveyard. The longer I spend here, trying to fathom its complexities, the more it laughs at me for my seriousness, and chides me for my lack of application.

But I have only had twenty-five years on this planet, I say in my defence. You have had more than two thousand.

Greece has made me feel as if I know nothing. As if I were born in a new place. As if my family are frauds and the ghosts whose language I cannot speak or understand are my real kin. I feel my lies so deeply embedded inside me, I do not know where or how to begin to extract them. These are the lies we are given at birth. About God. About knowing the truth despite evidence to the contrary. About feeling a connection to an idea that is truthful, namely the idea of cleansing.

I do not know what I mean by this. But I have an urge to clean something, someone, I do not know. I dream of the Magdalene washing Christ's feet. I think of the filth that stained Lucifer's hooves.

I look down and think of how far these boots of mine have travelled since my departure from England.

Cleansing. The word bounces inside me like a child's toy. Like a spinning top. Like the refrain in a song.

Bathing

Shall we bathe, Sir Thomas? The water looks inviting.

We have been following dusty paths across rocky fields, looking at ruins. The sea is even older than the most ancient crumbling temple but so shiny it looks new born.

Sir Thomas' face is very red and hot, despite the fresh breeze. He looks about. There is no one in sight.

I think, I would like to be naked here, beneath such a sky.

Why not, Richard. There is no one here.

We walk to the beach and take our clothes off, careful not to look at one another.

Then we are in the water.

It is cool and clear like glass.

The water wakes us up.

We both draw our breath in and then breathe out noisily.

The sky is curved and blue and does not move.

Everything is silent.

We walk into the water until it covers our chests.

I put my head beneath it and am baptised.

I have been immersed in ancient waters.

Gods swam here once.

We are clean now, if only momentarily.

Sir Thomas sighs with pleasure and holds his face up to the heavens and closes his eyes.

Mine have been opened so wide the light burns into them.

The Sea that Surrounds Greece

The sea is absurdly blue, a transparent, seductive place that is unlike any place I have ever seen. It is possible to watch an octopus converse with a mullet twenty feet below and to see the irritation in their eyes at the interruption of a boat.

Octopus is a delicacy here. The fishermen stand in a row and bash the poor creatures repeatedly until they have broken every muscle in their bodies. This violence apparently makes their meat very tender. The men chat together and smoke, while their arms flail up and down with indifferent, murderous intent.

But then I have also seen a fisherman cradle a dying fish and observed children dive deep into the blue and emerge with silver shells.

I have walked in the dim corridors of monasteries built from cliffs, raised from the sea.

I have seen islands appear from the faint, misted horizon, where the day before nothing existed but water. Even Sir Thomas has commented on this phenomenon. Land would seem to exist at whim in this singular country.

Such miracles make me reflect on the solid earth that gave birth to me, the predictable hills and sodden skies of Chatham. I have wondered if Chatham wasn't as equally magical as Greece, only more secretive in the manifestation of its magic. Such a confident god as Zeus never, after all, ruled it. I have wondered if landscapes can know one another, if they ever meet, and possibly converse in a common language, in another realm. I have tried to convey this thought to Sir Thomas, who, in his infinite simplicity, called me a fanciful artist to ask such questions. This, I tried to tell him, has no bearing on art whatsoever, but he would not listen. He would prefer not to have his experience of reality, which is what is really at stake, even slightly stirred.

The Parthenon

I have never seen marble breathe so violently in its death throes as I have in Athens. The Parthenon was sad enough to weep at, so empty of Gods it echoed with their absence as we walked up its steps. (Where do the Gods go when they die? Who buries the last dead God?)

The steps are lined with thin grooves.

An old woman approached me as I was examining them.

She was so stooped that to look at the ground was her natural posture.

Without further ado, and without asking me if I wished to know, she told me that these thin lines were carved into the stone to ease the passage of animals up to the heights of the temple for sacrifice. The grooves were there so their little hooves would not slip.

This made me feel very sad. Sir Thomas noticed my sadness and chided me.

Richard, you are too sentimental. Why, in England we slaughter beasts every day. You are happy to eat their flesh.

He is right. It is astonishing that I have never thought about the thoughts of the animals I eat. I could weep at my lack of compassion, which is only indicative of an even greater, widespread lack. We are a cruel culture, perhaps even crueller than the ancients, because we do not call our cruelty by its real name. We disguise the slaughter of our animals under the rubric of normalcy and need, and delight in accusing less hypocritical countries than our own of barbarism.

Rhodes

The steamer will not arrive and so we are stranded here, but it is less of an imprisonment than a stroke of luck. Sir Thomas leaves me alone to sketch and as a result I have achieved more in a few days here than I have in weeks on the road.

Being reunited with my pencil has returned normalcy to my hands. I did not realise how restless they had become.

The sun penetrates everything here, even when it is not hot.

The Gulf of Corinth

There are lost things in the water I cannot find. Jewels perhaps or lives even. Glances flung from the decks of anonymous boats, or handkerchiefs, or grapes. I believe I saw a small mirror drifting quietly beneath the surface of the sea, but it sank before I could be sure of what I had seen.

It is all I can do to lean as far as I can over the rail to peer even further.

In every wave a picture hides from me, but none I can mention or describe to my companion. The reasons for my reticence are manifold. Some of the objects I witness are indescribable, on account of their beauty. Others are too cruel for my imagination to accommodate. Some I would prefer not to believe are possible. Others, I must be honest, most, in fact, I do not have the vocabulary for. How is it possible to communicate thoughts that have not been shaped into an appropriate language?

This secrecy in me is beginning to tire even myself, and I would not persist if it were not necessary. But we are on our way to Delphi, and their lies are sure to be revealed. So I must keep quiet until we arrive.

I am anxious only on one count. I do not remember if withholding information constitutes lying.

But we will soon drink the inspiring waters of the Castalian Fountain.

Delphi

Alas! Whilst I have never before drunk from the Castalian Fountain, the sacred spring of Delphi, I recognise immediately how corrupted and defiled this place has become. Where Pythia, High Priestess of the Temple of Apollo, once bathed, is now a refuge for washerwomen, who shout their interminable filth with unrelenting energy. These holy waters are poisoned and sluggish, home only to frogs and watercress.

We walk the ruins, and again and again our footsteps echo with absence. The vanishing of past meanings, the lack of any replacement. The absence of any feeling between Sir Thomas and myself, and between Sir Thomas and me and the local people, who see us only as types. I see them look at us, convinced we are the same. It is enough to make me gag, to have myself associated with such a man. I attempt to distance myself from him, but cannot. His presence, even when he is not beside me, clings to me like a stain.

Delphi is the site of a vanquished army, a sad place of ruins. And not only the ruins of buildings, but also the ruins of hope. Religion has floated to the surface of this place and become a thing, not a spirit. Nothing will flourish here again. This is a rancid place.

Fictions

We have left Europe behind, and, for me, it was a sweet, if harrowing, departure.

The strangeness of travel is something I wish to embrace. I do believe I have to dive as deeply into its dislocation with the exuberance of the children we witnessed in Greece diving for sponges. Europe is a word I knew once, but now, it must be left behind. I have often understood a painting more profoundly when I have not seen it for a while. The abandonment of colour can allow content to be felt all the more keenly.

We are now in Africa and, without a moment's rest, have looked at stories carved into walls.

Sir Thomas does not realise their lack of fiction. For him they are exotic things, devoid of a life outside the sphere of the guidebook, the sketchbook, and the adventurer's tale. He does not realise they are not stories.

Time, I have discovered, is not a series of discreet rooms.

It is built by an invisible architect, who often makes his walls from water.

I wonder at Sir Thomas' growing distrust of me, which he would be the first to deny.

Have I become so transparent that he can sense my indifference to him?

Has he become so visually literate that the layer of skin that enfolds me has begun to reveal how thin a covering it is?

In the dark, my hands fly about and fill the void that surrounds me with line and then my still hands tremble on the counterpane. I feel the dilation of my pupils, the absorption rate of my eyes, denied their illumination.

I am no longer in a place that I recognise.

What Do I Draw?

My pencil has danced of late and would dance even faster if the sun would allow. My hand has become a choreographer who fills the space above the paper, the area that hovers perpetually between the eyes and the hand. It grabs the shapes and forms handed to me and places them gently on the page, where they rest, sun struck and soporific themselves.

What have I drawn?

The lights that fill me pour from windows, from the sky, from eyes; from sad candles that soften the moon's blow.

The light that slips through the crack in curtains.

The light of dew on leaves; the glow of broken porcelain, a sliver of glass, a splinter of polished wood. The light that slips from the dim half-light of tearooms, the markets, the mosaics in the corner of my room. The light that embraces people from behind, in doorways. The light in cloth, in the sweet, dark robes of the women, in the shade cloths, the cloth woven for the sole purpose of keeping out the very substance that gives it form.

The lovely figure of minarets, the precious cargo of secrets in every glance.

The sweep of a gown. Dust on a girl's neck. Variations on a theme of warmth. A sky like an eggshell. Swallowing streets. One donkey and then another. The difference between eyelids, curved eyes, the movement between a mouth and its relationship to the ear. The fall of youthful hair across a pockmarked cheek. A curl on the down of a baby's eyebrow. A rough elbow. The general hint of a belly. The ubiquity of bellies. A woman close to birth, her beautiful introspection. A sturdy leg on a delicate body. The bleaching of tones and bones, a scrubbed table.

The dilated pupils of a Priest.

The diluted sugar in a cup.

The colour of honey.

What do I draw?

The violent, yellow sand; the desert. The hypnotic lope of camels.

I draw boats made from hair lines, with flying spars. I draw their rigging, a series of connections, the points between, strung out, thin. I draw the light constantly denied me.

A Song

A thin, high song has been coming to me. It increases in volume as we travel. I suspect that this is because I am getting closer to it. I would love to tell Sir Thomas of my excitement. Or Maria. My father. I would like to share it with someone who could hear it too. But I cannot attempt to do so, because it is impossible to write a sound. It is not a song I have ever heard, and quite despite myself, when I first encountered it, it was so clear and so loud I asked Sir Thomas if he heard it too. He said not, and looked at me queerly and talked idiotically of cool drinks and shade.

I shook him off with a clear still eye and walked further up the worn steps to a place he could not go and pressed my ear to the stone and listened so hard, I thought my ears would bleed.

It was the sweetest sound and I know it sang for me. I could describe it in an image: imagine, if you will, bright yellow corn framed by a blue sky, the kind of sky you can't believe won't crack beneath the pressure of the sun. Now, imagine moving away from this place and quickly you are somewhere else. A red place, of soft light and whispering, but not of wicked origins. A good, a pure whispering, that makes the listener work to hear it.

That is a good description of the sounds I heard today.

A Conversation

We are resting, a rare moment, beneath some more ruins. I am sitting on a large, warm stone, attempting to draw. The desert is as simple as a picnic rug, but unfathomable in its combinations. How something so hard and dry can dissolve so gently into an image of water, which in reality is only more sand, is beyond me.

My pencil is fine and sharp. Lines link with other lines, gradually.

Sir Thomas is lying, resting, his arms flung out, his face stung with dust and exhaustion. He speaks suddenly, and for once his voice does not sound like a man giving a lesser man a lecture.

It sounds unusually sad.

This is all so old, Richard. So old.

I am about to ignore him, when something in his attitude stops me. He is still. His eyes are focussed, not roaming, not closed, but staring up at the ancient stones that rise above him. Even his voice is quiet. This has never happened before.

And so, I answer him.

Yes, Sir Thomas, they are old.

He is deep in some reverie. It is so mysterious; I cannot help but stare at his portly stillness.

Richard?

Sir Thomas?

What is the youngest thing you know?

He has thrown me.

Thing, Sir Thomas, or person?

Not even a pause, as if he has planned this conversation.

Whatever, Richard. Just something young.

A slight impatience litters his vowels, as if I, not he, am the obtuse one.

I think hard.

Eggs.

Silence. A loaded silence, which emanates from Sir Thomas, and which wishes for more from me. I struggle with the effort of speaking honestly to him.

A drawing just begun.

A sigh of satisfaction from Sir Thomas.

So, I think, this is where he was leading. To another dissection of the artistic impulse.

I groan. Out loud, without meaning to.

Without sitting up, or looking at me, Sir Thomas speaks sharply. Richard, you are too precious, sometimes, about something that is, after all, only lines rendered by a mortal on what was once something living. I mean paper, of course.

I am too astonished to reply.

He continues.

Tell me something else. Something else young. There is too much here that has suffered with age. It is tiring me today.

I think hard.

Spring. Every year, it's young again.

He doesn't reply, but a smile spreads across his face. He looks satisfied. Spring!

He laughs, stretches, resumes his silence, then sleeps.

I continue my attempt to capture the wilderness, in fine lines, for his album.

Night Again

Tonight we sit on our hotel balcony, high above the city.

It is a cool place to drink our brandy after supper. The lights of Alexandria, this mongrel bazaar they call Alexandria, are stretched before us. They look like wet seeds on velvet that shine and dance, but, in truth, today the whole world has danced for me as if it were fit to dance itself into the grave.

Considering its age, I wonder at its lack of exhaustion.

Comfortable on this balcony, the mouths of the city are hushed, its lights wild and abstract. Sir Thomas laughs that we are gods in the clouds, as we were in the mountains near the Rhine.

Ah, he sighs, remember how cool and clean the breeze was there? and sucks on his cheroot with a wistful face, as if he would rather be sitting on a brown bench with a cold ale and a red-cheeked girl than here, where the colours are built to break hearts and inspire homes for homeless words.

His large fingers drum the table beside him. He scratches his knee, as if ready to tear the cloth that covers it.

I do not laugh or sigh with him.

I could weep, the lights of the city are so glorious with their youthful, vivid complexions. And although so small and delicate and far away, it is easy to see now their real scale. Lights to be entered, lights of doorways, of windows, of spaces to hide in. I would have run down the steps and into the throat of the lanes and been swallowed gratefully by them, passed through their portals and frames, but Sir Thomas holds me back, with his jocularity and pedantry, his assumption that I will stay by him, that we will retire at a similar hour, eat breakfast together, look at the same things and respond with the same words, share the same thoughts.

He has me by the scruff of the neck; he has me tied to him, like the legs of a donkey are tied together to stop it running.

I am one leg, and he is another, but we are not the same beast. I feel very strongly the need for this fact to be reiterated. I have seen many a donkey hop to find shade.

It is easy to weep for donkeys.

Sir Thomas has tied me to him with his generosity, with his money, and even with his affection, he has tied me to him. I have, and this is true, occasionally and wildly looked about me for the nosebag.

To contradict him would take more energy than is worth my while, so I agree with him, for peace. It will have to do for the moment.

I will make pictures of our travels to satiate his appetite for evidence.

I sit quietly beside him, and we sip our brandy and talk of Home and archaeology, and I can feel the dust of countless digs settle on our words. I hear our voices from a distance, they are calm and measured. Some small bats fly behind him, he does not notice, I laugh and wave but only to myself, and imagine, even as I speak so calmly, the shadow of a flame on a wall.

The problems of Plato's cave.

Sir Thomas believes that he enters the Arab spirit when he puts on their robes, and does not see the girls snigger behind their narrow brown hands. He smokes water pipes with the face of a banker, and considers himself travelled.

There is something sly in his soul that I cannot trust, something not of the surface.

Speaking with Women

Everything I see was made by a man. I accompany a man in my travels and deal with men in carriages and hotels.

Although motherless, in my old familiar life women normally surround me. The lack of them has made me hungry for their company, despite the fact that they are secret people. They possess an intriguing and unique quality. Men rarely say what is on their minds, but at least you can ask them, however obliquely. Women demand propriety that I find exhausting. If only you could sit quietly with one, and simply look. I need to breathe one in, from a narrow distance.

So, I speak to her, a girl looking at the walls of a church. A young Englishwoman, who has wandered away from her aunt. I know what they are to each other because I have been listening to their conversation. The niece speaks of history, the aunt of luncheon. The niece sighs, her eyes drawn to the place around her, while the aunt does not listen and expresses a need to sit. The hair of the niece is lemon-pale and her skin is soft and slightly pitted.

I like the plum colour of her dress and the awkward angle of her shoulders, which twist slightly, as if a weight is pressing at her side.

As she gazes at the things around her, her small hands clutch a worn guidebook. Her eyes are never still. I would have called her mine then, but it may have startled her. We have not yet exchanged a word, but I know her heart. It is timid, but good, and slightly bored. There is a curiosity in it.

She is someone waiting for something that in all likelihood will never arrive.

It is a difficult thing to do, to choose the words to speak to a woman. So I decide on the simplest ones I can think of, the kind of words that would confuse no one.

Excuse me.

She turns and looks at me. Her eyes are blank, distracted. Polite. Yes?

I have lost my guide. May I glance at yours?

Certainly. She passes it over.

She says, here we are in page 67.

I laugh but realise that she does not intend to be funny, and so I duly turn to the aforementioned page and look at the words, which I do not read. Without looking up, I question her.

Have you been here long?

No. A week. We are headed for Thebes.

Ah. Thebes.

I imagine her naked. She is so pale and thin.

I blink hard.

She asks, have you been there?

Yes.

Did it interest you?

Yes.

I am warming to my subject when our intimacies are interrupted by a call from the aunt. We turn. The old harridan looks annoyed.

Grace. Come. It is time for lunch.

I hand her back her book. She looks at me. Her eyes, for a moment, do not move from mine.

She coughs a little.

Goodbye.

I bow. Goodbye.

Grace.

And then she is gone.

Such finality in so brief an encounter.

How is it possible to hold the attention of a woman?

They are always in the thrall of someone else.

The ruin is empty now and I am hungry.

So I leave.

The Impossibility of Sleep

My bed is too hot. The sheets slip off my skin. I am made of eggshell. At night I wake and see small lizards fly through the night heat.

The moon is appropriate here. It is not like the moon of Suffolk Street, nor the moon of Chatham. England has a cold moon, a moon with pronounced vowels, a restrained moon. Here the moon is as violent as such a city must demand.

Someone has beaten this moon, so it shines like a bruise, like something recovering, and it bleeds through my window and begs me to press something on it, to cool it.

I dreamt God's fist smashed into bronze and tossed the result away. Tossed into the sky, the moon a failed plate, a repository of fury, a shiny, lost thing.

It comes at me and I cannot bear to look up. It falls on this terrible, slippery cloth covering my hot body, and it is unbearable.

The moon forces me to walk at night, to leave my bed, until I can recognise the moon I used to know, the cold and lovely one that huddles beneath the hot one here.

I can hardly remember the way it used to look, but am reminded when my thoughts have become as calm and as clear as the light it used to offer.

I slip out of our hotel and walk, because walking is the only activity that wills still my giddy head, my restless body.

The sounds draw me in before the images, the crying and laughing and sighing and wheels and hooves and soft treads of camels, the hints of lives unseen but heard, that stain and animate every crack of every Alexandrian breath. The Egyptian night falls suddenly and all objects become shadows. I walk through the midnight heat of the city as if it were a wall I must break down with every step. The heat throbs from every cobblestone, rising from the black water of the port, and then dropping like boiling sparks from the immense stars that litter the sky so beautifully and so ominously. I have read that shooting stars are stones thrown by the angels in heaven to drive off evil, eavesdropping djinns. They must be parasitical in their eavesdropping, then never have I seen so many bright flashes across the sky. Heaven must be an active place, curious about its bed linen, the earth. It is difficult, however, to read such strange beauty. A shooting star is as violent and as shocking to witness as a gunfight in a forest at night.

The heat rises from the bowels of the earth. The ground feels as if it has been warmed by hell itself, drugged and burnt by Lucifer. The smells of humans and animals intermingle. Sometimes it is difficult to tell the two apart.

Women of every colour greet me in doorways, copper women, like furnaces, cool lemon-coloured women, earth-coloured women, gold and black and painted women. They mumble and murmur and entreat me as I pass down narrow streets and I do not dignify them with a response. This city does not know who or what it is, a temple, a sacrificial altar, a meeting place, a church, a sacred place or a hideously profane one.

It changes its mind at every street corner. Copts, Greeks, Jews, Moslems, Turks and Armenians, threadbare camels with hideous grins, humble donkeys, starving cats and mildewed dogs, bejewelled whores and naked saints. The sun and the moon, the sea and the desert live side by side as if their origins were simply ingredients for this enormous dish that has produced Alexandria.

Confusion builds in my head like malformed bricks build an unstable house. I try to comprehend such a place, but am too mute and deaf to decipher such complex and, despite the surface of this place, often-invisible information that is proffered.

I remain both literally and metaphorically in the dark.

I have become a night man, a moon man, an insomniac.

The sea front offers me some respite, gay as it is with light and the sloping lines of its low horizon. The sea is as smooth as a young girl's cheek that swells occasionally with something sucked and sways to a vague plume of music. In this place I can sit and drink mastic after mastic and feel the sea breeze stroke my head like a friend and watch the ships pull in and out and be reassured that whatever the vagaries of my imagination, and however unsettled this place may have made me, there is always the ocean and the leave-taking it offers. Also, the antics of the sailors, sailors from places so far-flung I cannot identify their languages, offer me some amusement. They row ashore from their ships and immediately acquire at least one woman and copious bottles of alcohol and usually interrupt their carousing to cram their mouths and bellies full of squid, cuttlefish or pigeons. I have seen women laughing as they lick the juice from the sailors' unshaven chins, and seen a tongue covered with fish juice enter a painted mouth. These are scenes from Dante or Bosch. How I wish I were a Shakespeare to give them the descriptions, the moral context and the narrative they demand. But I am not. I am simply, and I say this with gorge in my throat, I am simply a scribbler of lines, of outlines and surface.

Like a dilettante, I observe the play but always leave before the final act. As a writer my observations are impotent. But as an artist, they are simply waiting for my interrogation.

I am distracted by the bricks in every building, distracted by the hand of the person who placed them there. I am crushed by their anonymity. I pass the open door of a home.

Who plucked those flowers, who crushed the corn?

I need to follow people, to learn who they are.

As the sailors and their whores stumble from tavern to tavern, their voices and songs become louder and louder, their cheeks more violently coloured, their hearts painfully more aggressive and amorous. I have delighted in following certain couples over the course of one night. At times, I have not been able to return to my hotel, despite bone-numbing exhaustion, because I have been compelled to wait for the next instalment, the next kiss, fight or leave-taking. These players in my never-ending one-act play have become my mental acquaintances, and I have had to remind myself that they do not know me as I know them, as they dance and float past me with their sly floozies, pursued by clouds of aromatic smoke and nauseating scent. I have had to hold my hands tight in my lap so as not to greet them as old friends. I try to draw them before the mastic has become my employer, when my mind is not too overwrought. I find a certain peace in the control my pencil offers me.

I slip back to the hotel before Sir Thomas awakes, splash cold water on my face and appear before him for breakfast, pretending I have slept as soundly as he.

Over sweet, warm rolls and coffee, he has begun to comment on my pale cheeks and trembling hands, to see through my protestations of wellness. He has requested I take a sleeping draught.

He will never learn of my night rambles. I cannot tell him. He may try to make me give them up, but I will not give them up, however tired I might be.

I will never sip his sleeping draught.

I may never wake up.

Lust

Sir Thomas and I hurry through the streets of Alexandria. Deserted trees huddle together like naked lunatics in the silent squares. I shy away from them in fright.

Please, Richard. We are in a hurry. Hurry.

Poinsettias stain a wall. Fugitive pockets of heat slap me intermittently. The night, and our purpose, has made me acutely aware of shadows.

I do not know why we are in such a hurry. I cannot imagine that whores are particular about time. But Sir Thomas is increasingly impatient with me. It is easy for a man with no imagination and no moral imperative to become irritated. If I was not so right and he so wrong I would be irritated with me also.

Sir Thomas was loathe to include me in his little outing, but was forced to do so when I interrupted his conversation with Hamid (a Nubian Sir Thomas has employed to show us the Real World of the Arab), and he did not pretend that I had not heard. I heard him as clear as daylight, as anyone would. The trembling undercurrent of his voice makes it clear – he is feeling lascivious.

He has patiently explained to me that the reasons for his visit are purely anthropological.

In that case, Sir Thomas, thank you, I would be glad to come. Perhaps I will gain some material. For a painting.

He looks slightly aghast at the thought, and the ensuing expression in his eye makes me aware of his lack of invitation, but an imp has entered my soul and I return his gaze with limpid eyes.

I am filled with curiosity. I am old enough now.

I would like to touch a woman, and, if possible, to forget myself for a while.

I have not, of course, expressed my desires so bluntly to Sir Richard, but continue simply to articulate my purely academic interest at viewing, at first hand, the contemporary Alexandrian whorehouse. But Richard, your father ...

My relationship with my father, Sir Thomas (and I speak with almost as much pomposity as he is wont to address me), is a matter between that good gentleman and myself. I am an adult, Sir Thomas. If you hadn't noticed.

He glares at me with his bulbous eyes. He cannot retract his conversation. That would negate the angle of his anthropological argument. Imp roars inside me with glee.

All right, Richard, if you insist. Tonight, at midnight. Hamid will take us. He coughs and concentrates on a distant spot on a nonexistent wall.

And please, Richard, do not, despite what you have just said, I ask you especially not to mention this excursion to your father. He may not fully understand our interest. He has never been here. He does not know the (coughs) customs.

I laugh quietly, but am stopped by a fierce look.

Of course not, Sir Thomas.

I cannot think of certain sections of his body without shuddering.

He drinks more than is his usual wont tonight. His cheeks are burnished red brown. His hands cannot keep still. He has placed his silkiest, most opulently coloured cravat around his neck and, speaks to me with averted eyes and a touch of fever about Egyptian representations of the cat. His sentences are pregnant with words he does not speak.

What will happen in this house?

Before we leave I escape to my room for a moment in a futile bid to gather my thoughts, which, I realise, at this moment, are ungatherable.

The excursion begins with knock on my door. It occurs to me that this journey with Sir Thomas could be mapped with the impressions of a thousand different knocks.

Richard. Are you ready? Time. It is time, boy.

Time. I open my door. He looks away. We meet Hamid in the foyer, who strides ahead, gesturing occasionally with his right hand for us to hurry, hurry.

Faces carved from a material more like stone than flesh pass us, hidden in heavy robes. Some glance at us, dull, shining, gemlike, and murmur obscene guttural sounds in our direction. I glimpse currant eyes in a suet pudding face, a hand clutched to a chest, an earring. The smell of these men reaches out to touch me; they reek of overripe flowers.

Our footsteps sound loud compared to people in robes and slippers. My body feels coarse and heavy, my lips thin and puritanical. I repeat to myself, I am a man in Alexandria walking towards an assignation with a whore.

It is difficult to recognise myself in myself.

I have just realised this: it is not necessary to understand the words these robed men utter, the sounds of the words are articulate enough, full as they are with lust and hate. This is all I need to know. After all, they would not be offering us tea at this late hour. More likely it is their sisters they would serve to us. But why do they murmur and pass on when they must know we cannot respond? What do they want us to do?

How would they wish us speak to them?

I have heard the songs of the funeral women, the high-pitched, frightened gurgling that spins around their mouths and eyes. I do not know the words of these songs, but they do not feel as sinister as these sly intimations of cruelty.

Their faces make me long for a candle, or something familiar, light.

A pen, perhaps.

Wheels crash over ruts in the road. A man curses and it sounds like spitting. The thin, high-pitched whinnying of a beaten mule, the squeak and jangle of a harness.

Appropriate sounds to accompany such an assignation.

Hamid turns and gestures, hurry, hurry, and glides even faster along the uneven road.

A girl cries out from a shadow and is as suddenly quiet. I pray the hand across her mouth is gentle. Why did she cry out? I slow down to look. Imagine Maria or Sarah in such a situation. Jane!

But they are a different species.

Sir Thomas can hardly contain his anxiety.

Richard, please, do not look at them, it is not our business.

You do not know how angry they might become if they saw us looking.

We must hurry.

I am filled with a sudden desperate need to see something that will reveal God to me in these Arabic eyes, a God whose name is different from mine, but who is a God nonetheless. I have questions to ask Him.

Are we different? Would you spurn us? How could we know you? Would you truly burn us in eternity for our lack of love for you? Would you enjoy conversing with someone like me? Would you rather me dead than imaginative?

This city watches us from beneath its eyelids. It is more secretive than sleepy. I can sense the knives under the mattresses. How could a man become righteous or even good in such a city? Perhaps it is easy when the enemy is so tangible.

Sir Augustine. St Augustine. If he were born now would he still want in strength to resist temptation? Would he have visited such a place with Sir Thomas?

Hamid stops suddenly and gestures us towards a narrow door. It is unmarked. He knocks on it, and mumbles a response to the enquiry the door has offered. The door swings open. Sir Thomas clears his throat rapidly, three times. Hamid disappears inside. We follow.

A one-eyed midget in a turban is blocking our way. In the place of his missing eye, he has a flap of pink, trembling skin. He has crossed his arms across his chest and thick muscles and a large tattoo dominate his shoulders. One tattoo is a picture of a tiger in the act of leaping, and the other is a simple blue circle. I am already in such a state of disorientation that the appearance of this small man seems perfectly logical.

I would like to ask him why he chose these particular images for his limbs, but he glares at us out of his one eye, and then steps aside to let us through. I do not think he would like to talk with me about himself. I feel as if he has printed our faces on his mind's eye. His muscles are shaped for vengeance. He has the appearance of a man in whose robes a vicious implement might be concealed.

The corridor is narrow and long and dimly lit. Hamid walks down it with the air of a man who has walked this way before. The air is thick with incense and some other smell I find hard to place. I imagine I am in the bowels of a strange church, a catacomb, a place for hiding, a place of dreadful dreams. I would like to turn and run back, but cannot. We reach another door, and the three of us, Hamid, Sir Thomas and I, are momentarily pressed against each other, like survivors or escapees, waiting. Then the next door swings open.

My first impression is of a mad pool. Everything is blue. The dim wall is marked with the imprint of hundreds of small hands. I am shocked at first. I believe the marks to be from bloody hands, held out while the victims were dragged away. I begin to shake. Then I remember. They are imprints to repel the evil eye. I should find them reassuring but do not. They have left the idea of amputation in my head that, for a moment, I cannot dissolve. The floor is covered with rugs and cushions of quite extraordinary brilliance, the cloth woven from jewels and stars. The red is tempered with ultramarine blue, and yellow ochre and sap green, but the red dominates. Where it touches the other colours it trembles with particular brilliance. Candles glow from hidden points in the wall. And on every cushion reclines, sits up, dances, lies back, giggles a girl, girls I can hardly bring myself to describe they are so young and bizarre to me. Well-dressed, fattish, soporific men, who do not notice us and hardly seem capable of speech, paw many of the girls. Some girls sway to the sounds of a large elaborate instrument, which looks like a deformed guitar, played by a sightless old man in a dim corner. His hands move about as if someone else controlled them. His eyes roll upwards.

I cannot help but think of a marionette and check the ceiling for strings, but there are none. The music is mesmerising. It does not sound like a song with a beginning, middle or an end, but rather like the continuum of something snatched from the air. The girls dance in front of this blind musician, smiling at each other, giggling silently, touching their breasts and mocking his inability to witness their cruelty. Their legs are covered in elaborate silks that sway and shimmer with every movement. Their little breasts are naked beneath transparent beads, and bounce like soap bubbles as they dance. They have lined their eyes with charcoal. Some eyes are dull and glazed, some too animated for reason. Their dancing lacks joy, but not contentment. Their hips circle round and round like lazy hoops. Their hands build sculptures out of atmosphere.

These girls are probably the same age as my sisters.

I look away. There is nothing to see but the implication of lust on every surface in every corner, however small. What did I expect? My eyes, quite without my permission, drag my head around the room. It is as if every girl is identical, but within each repetition of a girl there is a sublime and subtle difference. They wriggle and writhe like exotic fish. As they gasp for air, some smile, or look tired, while others kiss men who lie almost prostrate in their arms, clutching water pipes. The air is thick with a sweet, sickly smoke.

Sir Thomas coughs gently and puts on his anthropological face. Opium, Richard. It is best to keep clear of it. If you are unused to it, it may make you sick. It may make you hallucinate apparitions you do not desire.

He speaks with his familiar, lecturing tone, as if his voice might afford this extraordinary scene some degree of normalcy.

Our gazes return to the girls. They are so young that the rouge on their cheeks gives them the appearance of dolls and the fur between their legs is like the fur of newborn kittens. Their hair has been curled, so it frames their little faces like halos. Their lips are painted a vivid, murderous red. Their arms are covered with bracelets that chime and jangle sweetly with their every movement.

An old woman enters from a door and comes up to us. She is limping, grinning and bejewelled. Her face is as soft as an old purse. She holds a limpid, sparkling girl in each hand. I realise Hamid is nowhere to be seen. The girls she holds look at us with boiling little eyes. Sir Thomas clears his throat five times. The old hag wordlessly puts a hand in one of ours. Sir Thomas is uncommonly silent. I wonder when he will start measuring and interviewing her, but he has been rendered deliciously mute and can only gaze at the exquisite little flower who has taken his hand with the expertise of an ancient courtesan.

I look at mine, this child I am buying, and could momentarily weep with shame and confusion. A tiny pink tongue comes out of her mouth and she licks her lips. She moves close to me and presses herself against my chest. My arms, without my permission, circle her body and reciprocate her embrace. She appears to be quite happy to be given to me. I do not know what is happening. She smells as hot as honey. Sir Thomas has disappeared. My eyes are too occupied to see anything but her burning little eyes.

Who set fire to this child that she should burn so?

She reaches up and licks my cheek. Her tongue cuts my flesh like a razor. I can do nothing to stop her licking me. She takes my hand with confidence and leads me to another door, a darker door, and we pass through it. A candle is placed on a candleholder every few inches along this corridor. It is as unreal as any place I have ever seen.

I feel like a flea moving along the neck of a queen.

She leads me to a door and we pass through it, all without a word, and the room she brings me to is small and flickering and filled with the smells of so many flowers I cannot breathe until she pushes me down, onto a deep, dark cushion and places her mouth onto mine, and fills my lungs with air from her body. Her hair falls across my face.

It smells of a heavy oil I do not recognise.

I do not know her name.

Her hair obscures her eyes. I look beneath the painted surface of her face. She has a small crooked mouth, a chipped tooth. A terrible, youthful, inquisitive expression lies deep in her eyes, tempered by something so tired and old I close my eyes, to make it disappear. When I open them, I am confronted with a tiny scar on her earlobe. I look and discover a mole on her neck, and a single white hair, in the midst of all the blackness on her head. I am filled with an overwhelming sense of doubt as to this girl's identity and age. I must see her as God made her. I sit up and she does the same, and puts her small brown hands on my chest. I push her away. We sit on the cushions, and stare at one another. Her eyes do not budge from mine. She licks her lips. I do not respond. I am sure this may be wrong, but would like, at this moment, to suspend such a judgement.

I command her to remove her clothes, her beads, and her jewels. At first she does not understand and leans into me, murmuring a low guttural sound like a cat with human eyes. I push her away, again and again.

Her eyes dart about the room as if she has lost something. I cannot risk it. I do not know what she may be hiding. I force her to stand up. She stands in front of me as limp as a rabbit skin, her eyes lowered and still. She holds out her arms in front of her as I slide her bracelets from her little wrists.

I undress her. She does not help me. She is just a girl. There is nothing hidden on her but her heart and her thoughts, which she is welcome to. I try the door, and look on the other side of it. No one is there. I return to the girl, who is still standing in the same position, and lie down. She lies beside me. She strokes my head and wraps her narrow brown arms around me. I am then inside her and she undoes me. She is gentle and moans and then whispers something I do not understand. But I do know one thing, and that is that she is on my side. For a moment I am deluded into thinking that I know where that is.

How We Speak of Lust

The next morning Sir Thomas and I are as correct with each other as bishops at breakfast.

Our mutual formality continues without respite for the next few days, until the memory of our nocturnal visit fades.

I wonder about his experience of that place we went to, and of which, in truth, I am unable to consider in a calm manner. Despite the fact that perfumed, somewhat horrifying images return to me again and again, I resist talking of it to myself.

But I am curious: did Sir Thomas treat that girl like a subject, like a specimen, like a curio or a hole, or did he lie beside her and look at her, his eyes on hers, and hers on his, one human to another? We will never speak of it; I know this for a certainty. I am entirely complicit. What happened that night no longer exists as something concrete.

It has entered a realm inside me to which I cannot go with anyone else. I am sure we have begun to believe that we did not go there. It was two other men in a different time.

But we can speak of the sphinx, even though it is far more mysterious and uncommon than lust. There is lust in every moment in every person's heart, acted upon, or frustrated, or incomplete, or violent. It is no different from breathing, yet no one would blush to discuss the mechanics of a breath.

I laugh privately and long at this. At the things we allow ourselves to think and not to think. We are master censors of our own minds.

The sphinx is as rare as married virginity. I am not convinced it was built from manpower. It is as unsettling an apparition as any I have witnessed, but also organic, as correct in its shape and form as sand.

But even knowing how right it is, I do not understand. It was made for a people who spoke with a different tongue than mine, whose minds were affected by stories I have not heard. It has upset me in all the thoughts I thought I understood so well, that held me upright and made me feel I knew my way around my own head. Travel is, perhaps, useful in that it prompts my own imagination to greater heights, greater exertions, but none the less, my soul is pervaded with a feeling of unease. My head and heart have become tattered maps, places where the ink has run, yet no one has appeared to clarify the routes this traveller should take. I think of my paintings and am not so convinced now of their fiction. This is a frightening thought. Here, I feel that with every glance in any direction, I take something that does not belong to me. As if my admiration trivialises the most superficial qualities these countries have to offer, namely, their surfaces.

My head is so full of terrible thoughts that at times I have truly doubted my own reason.

I have begun to believe that paintings are not imaginary things, while the world I move through is constructed entirely from shadows.

Convinced of Pursuit

I am enjoying the lemon stall when I first notice him. I feel him looking at me, as clearly as when you hear your name spoken in the babble of a crowd.

There is no reason for anyone to be so interested in me, to gaze at me from such close proximity, so why is he there? And why with his face covered? Why does he raise his hands constantly to his face, as if to brush something away? He has no need for lemons, that much is apparent. I do not imagine he is an artist; he somehow appears too distracted in things other than himself. Do men here simply step out to buy lemons? He does not carry himself like a servant. Is he a cook, perhaps?

But why would a cook look so furtive?

I do not mention his presence to Sir Thomas, who is exclaiming like a girl over the red of the tomatoes, the deep purple of the peppers. This man has made me indifferent to colour, too preoccupied, too worried about my safety. Is it this man's intention to rob me? Or worse?

Does he wish me dead?

Has someone sent him to spy on me?

I cannot mention his presence to Sir Thomas. He would fuss, and this dreadful shadowy man would notice and increase the deception of his sly behaviour. He is a problem I must handle on my own.

It is intolerably hot, and the noises are intense and overwhelming. Sweat pours from the end of my nose. There is a dog howling somewhere, men arguing, women wailing, a bell ringing, someone running fast from something, a million people haggling over a million rotting things.

I would like the noise to be dulled if only for a moment, so I might collect my thoughts and pack them away somewhere safe.

I am so hot I feel dizzy. My blood burns my veins, my feet in their shoes. I feel as though I must have baked my hands in an oven. My skin is wet with heat. I lift the brim of my hat and mop it with my handkerchief.

I would like to stand, just for a moment, in a London downpour without an umbrella, and shiver with cold.

I would like to lie in a cool, still dark room, with my eyes closed and have Maria bring me some water. But she is too far away, and I am here now, with a problem to attend to.

I am all too aware of the blood pumping through my temples, and through my brain. I do not enjoy the percussion of its passage.

I breathe the thick, slimy air deep into my lungs.

I spend a while choosing a lemon, to test where he will go. He does not move, but stays close to me, without a word.

Perhaps I should speak to him. But that is what he wants, he wants to have me somehow, it will give him a way in. I shall not utter a word in his presence.

I pause. He pauses. I buy lemons; he examines them and chooses one for himself.

Richard, what on earth do you need with lemons?

Sir Thomas by my side, reassuringly bluff. He is genuinely amazed. For a still life, Sir Thomas.

He laughs, relieved and solicitous.

Perhaps, boy, you would like some other fruit, as well?

No, I will do well enough with lemons.

I move through the souk, and pause at a perfume stall. Sir Thomas wanders at my side, gazing about him, making small observations, enjoying himself.

The colours of this place Richard!

I feel the man near me, his breath on my neck. I cannot turn to look at him. I will not.

We enter a narrow corridor of stalls. The air is suddenly and wonderfully full of flowers, sweet, fresh flowers. We are in the aisle of perfume sellers.

I am momentarily distracted. Sir Thomas covers his nose with his kerchief. Goodness, Richard. It is a little too much.

I tell him I would like to buy some scent for my sisters. They would enjoy the novelty.

I can see Maria's dark head bent, sniffing, exclaiming. Her brown eyes laughing with pleasure. A bottle of crushed roses. Some liquid gardenia. A drop of hot patchouli oil.

Sir Thomas thinks it a charming idea.

But this strange man is near. I cannot think of scent, or Maria, or even the possibility of London with this man in my orbit. A group of children materialise, they cluster around us begging, grabbing at our clothes, holding their filthy paws in front of them, palms up towards us with biblical supplication. I brush them away and they return again and again. Ignore them Richard, they will get bored. It is the best way. Ignore them. I cannot.

I ask them politely to leave me be. They will not. I ask them again and again but they feign incomprehension. I shout suddenly at them and am surprised at the rage in my voice. They scatter like ants before a fire. Sir Thomas turns at my anger and looks at me with anxious eyes.

He takes my arm. Without thinking, I shake him off. I am abrupt. Sir Thomas looks even more anxious.

Richard, you must not let these children irritate you so. We will have to deal with many more before our journey is ended. You must learn compassion and detachment.

From the man who stamped on the toes of a child!

He is right, for once, but his lack of memory inspires in me a desire to smash my fist into his face.

I am too hot. I need to be cool. I am too hot.

I will see you up ahead, Richard. I will be at the carpet stalls.

He is disappointed in me.

I will join you shortly, Sir Thomas.

My voice hovers above me. I doubt it belongs to me.

Shopkeepers entreat me, children grab again and again at my clothes, with their incessant demands of baksheesh.

The perfume stall is a tiny, narrow room, filled with hundreds of wooden drawers that stretch high up to the ceiling. An old man in a long white robe greets me and ushers me in. Without a word he pours me a cup of tea. The angle of his hand as he lifts the cup, the delicacy with which he begins to pour makes me want to weep.

I turn around. I see the man from the lemon stall peering intently in at me. I turn suddenly, back to the perfume shop owner and am overcome with waves of nausea. I put my head between my knees. When I straighten up, the old man is looking at me with an imperturbable expression. He passes me a cup of sweet, fragrant tea and I sip it. It calms me.

The man murmurs words to me I do not understand, but his face is kind and my head cools.

I do not dare to turn around again.

Productivity

Sir Thomas finishes his letter with a flourish, sits back and lights his pipe. Hamid approaches him. He orders a brandy, glances over at me and orders one for me as well. I think he prefers my company slightly drunk. I busy myself with drawing. I draw the chairs, the tiles, the fingernail of moon through the arched window. My pencil flies about like a firefly. I am simply the passenger on its back. I cannot talk to Sir Thomas at the moment. We stumble about in conversation like peasants wearing clogs trying to make their way through a muddy field. His letters Home are a constant reminder to me of the purpose of our trip. Of why I am here with him and he with me. We are here to see other cultures, to try and understand them and to take Home with us what we have seen, quite despite the fact that we cannot understand anything that anyone has said to us, and quite despite the fact that we are insensitive to these peoples' gods, I know Sir Thomas feels the supremacy of his own, and although I struggle against it, I cannot help but feel something in me that is equally patronising to our hosts.

What can Sir Thomas' reasons be for such displacement? He professes a passion for travel and is known as a traveller, but all I see in his face as he walks through a foreign place is another little piece of England.

When he talks to me, it is as if someone had taken a bell from a village church in Hampshire and rung it from a mosque. His face, the words he speaks, the movement of his body through this foreign place, is so strange, that occasionally they endear me to him. He is as dislocated as I am, and in that, at least, we are comrades.

Whereas I feel uncomfortable when I look on the face of the sphinx, dwarfed by my ignorance of its function, Sir Thomas admires the manpower that could create such a thing. He treats history like a book he is keen to finish. He treats these people as if they were no more than subjects for pictures. As if their history stopped at the same point as their skin.

The Desert

I have been told that the Egyptians believe the desert to be an emptiness populated entirely by the spirits of demons and other grotesque visitants from Eblis, the Moslem Lucifer. I have an urge to see such a desolate place for myself and not trust to superstition what I might be able to ascertain, or understand, with reason.

(But is it possible, a voice in my head whispers, to see such a devil? His disguises would be a hundredfold more skilful than your imagination.) Sir Thomas is excited at our imminent adventure.

We set out at dawn, Sir Thomas, Hamid and I, accompanied by a swathed and taciturn guide whose name I cannot grasp. We are mounted, for once, on noble animals, delicate Arab ponies that look as if they have actually been fed and cared for. Mine is dappled grey and gazes at me with startled eyes. Before I mount, I whisper him endearments, and he nuckers in response and mumbles his soft lips across my palm, licking the salt in my sweat. Despite his Arab origins, I do not doubt he can understand me. He stands as still as a hill as I mount. I lean down and stroke his neck, and his ears flicker back and forward, listening, looking all around.

If the devil exists in the desert, this pony will warn me, I am sure of it. He has a wise little dished head, and curved, lovely ears. His eyes are good and watchful. He has fast, fragile legs. I am proud to travel this way, on such an intelligent beast.

Our heads are wrapped in a cloth, Bedouin fashion. I feel slightly absurd, but Sir Thomas is as proud as an explorer.

One for the sketch book, Richard! he cries and strikes a heroic pose. I laugh despite myself.

The air is still cool and dim, the minarets of the mosques glazed with dew.

Hamid has told me desert people carry the map of the desert in their heads and orientate themselves at night by the stars.

And by the sun? I ask. He looks at me queerly.

And the sun he replies.

The only day star, the sun.

We pass beyond the long shady plantations and small lakes until we reach the final gasping borders of cultivation, a border that pockmarks the country with pestilence. It is damp and stinking and humid. Sir Thomas rides with one hand, the other holding a handkerchief to his face, his eyes shining above it like hard, glazed stones. Hamid's face is still and forward looking, as if he does not need to breathe unless he chooses to. Our silent guide rides ahead, without ever once looking back at us, without ever once raising his hands to his face.

I refuse to hold anything to my nose, despite Sir Thomas' entreaties.

I will smell this country as closely as I choose to look at it. But it sticks to my throat like tar. The taste of rotting fish coats my tongue.

We trot by a fetid marsh of giant reeds and bulrushes. The sky is as empty as a locked waiting room. The birds have left, or perhaps were never here at all. Fish float dead with white eyes on the vile salt and slime-encrusted surface. The desert, it would seem, likes to greet growth with a dead embrace.

Then we are past it, the ponies treading as delicately as dancers in a bog. The sky is tinged with lilac. The desert air crowds around us, ebullient, abruptly fresh. Its clean breath slakes and cleanses our gagging throats. Sir Thomas stuffs his handkerchief in his pocket and beams at the sky, his face held up to the sun like a sacrificial bowl.

Ah Richard, the air he cries.

Yes, Sir Thomas, the air.

It is all around us. I have never been surrounded by such solid air.

We leave behind a no man's land of arid land cracked with wildflowers and shifting butterflies. Suddenly, the earth changes, and a limitless canvas, a blue expanse of sky undercut with raw pale sand presents itself to us. Our nameless guide breaks, without warning, into a gallop. We follow him joyfully, plunging through the soft dunes with the jerky machinations of wild marionettes. Such a naked expanse should feel like a wasteland but does not. It is not desolate. It is a distilled place, as beautiful as a stream of milk.

Our horses pant and strain for breath, foam pours from their nostrils and their sides heave with the staccato effort of their movement through space. The horizon trembles with mirages. Sweat pours down my face and makes my vision tremble even more. I wonder if my horse can see the mirage. My shirt sticks to my back.

I feel more alive in this desert than I ever have anywhere in my life.

I know what it means to be a centaur.

We ride to a small oasis, huddled beneath a large unexpected rock. It appears in the heat like a vision and looks to my mind like a dog's head. Ohh! Ohh! cries Sir Thomas.

Three palm trees and a small pool have never been more warmly greeted by a former mayor.

Our horses drink, their flanks heave in and out like bellows, and we sit on the cushions Hamid has brought us. Our guide will not look at us, he faces away, across the sand as we nibble on dates and curd cheese and sip sweet, cold tea. Hamid is in a sombre mood. Perhaps he is suspicious of the desert, but if he is he will not tell us. Instead he tells us stories of the smugglers' roads between Algiers and Mecca, highways he says smell of spices and blood, highways of camel tracks that have remained unchanged for hundreds of years despite the shifting dunes. He tells us, his voice hushed in awe, of sheikhs' tents as large as mansions, erected in the middle of the desert, made from cloth woven out of goat hair. He tells us of the Arabic fear of blue eyes and red hair. I look at Sir Thomas, at his thinning, greying red hair and watery blue eyes and laugh and laugh. Sir Thomas becomes disgruntled and I have to backtrack, work hard to alleviate his bad temper. Hamid continues looking down at his crossed feet as he talks. This combination of elements, he murmurs, red hair and blue eyes, are considered evil signs in the Koran, a fact consolidated by the repulsive features of examining angels, who are marked by both.

Sir Thomas scratches his head nervously and coughs again.

So, Hamid.

Yes, sir?

Do I make you nervous?

No, sir. You are English.

Good, good.

Sir Thomas is relieved. He does not seem to have noticed that Hamid did not look at him as he spoke and muttered something in Arabic after his dismissal of Sir Thomas' potential to be the embodiment of evil.

More tea, Richard?

Thank you, Sir Thomas. I will.

Hamid jumps up to check the horses. Our silent guide does not move. Sir Thomas and I lie beneath the palm trees and look at the sky.

It is inevitable that we fall asleep in such heat, in such silence. We sleep and we sleep and we sleep. And as I sleep I have a terrible nightmare, but I do not remember what it is that frightens me.

I wake up screaming. Sir Thomas appears at my side, slaps my face gently and holds a water bottle to my lips. I think of Michelangelo's Pieta. I can smell Sir Thomas' English shaving soap. It is almost stranger than my dream to smell such a smell in such a place, in an oasis.

I sit up and am quiet. I cannot speak. I am chilled to my core.

Sir Thomas says, enough heat for you my boy, and enough superstitions for one day. No wonder you had a nightmare. Dreadful stories.

He snorts softly.

Hamid looks away, then takes a small phial out of his satchel and brings it to me. Wordlessly he takes the stopper out and holds it to my nostrils. The scent of jasmine.

I breathe it in deeply and it calms my nerves.

Our guide is kneeling, looking away from us, muttering incantations. La Illah Illa Allah. No God but one God.

The Unsent Letter Home

My Dear Family,

I must clarify something to you, which I do not believe I have made clear.

When I speak of myself as an artist, you must understand that by artist I mean a person consumed with an enthusiasm too big for containment. The impulse to create something from the interaction of the mind with the world must colour every decision the artist makes. But, conversely, the concept of decision is a fluid one. Often, the artist (the good artist) feels as if there are no decisions, only extreme forms of cause and effect. As for myself, I should really fear to write to any of you about how much I feel when I see all of these treasures that the earth has revealed to me, and that I have only so lately witnessed: cities as big and as strange as mountains, or enormous clouds or the deep blue of the sky. In the alleys of these cities, in the chasms and gorges of these mountains, beneath the thick, hot scrub of the plains, in the restraint of the desert and in the sparkling and shadowed detachment of the sky: in these places the brightest colours of the symbols of eternity are to be found.

My enthusiasm betrays me into writing what it would puzzle me to explain: namely, that to be here makes my heart expand, and to dwell amongst such places is to be confronted by thoughts as great and as mysterious as the sand and sky and stone themselves.

I content myself fanning the flames the world has placed before me.

I wait patiently. I know it will not be long before this fire alters forever the shape of the enigmas in my mind.

Cairo

Decrepit horse cabs pull veiled women through the narrow streets. I do not notice the men. The veils of the women make me curious.

The attentive desert waits in the air, and insinuates itself in particles that wedge in my eyes. My head feels as empty as the rooms of some great abandoned mansion. I am exhausted but cannot sleep. Everyone around me is either moving towards something or someone. I have become inert and can only watch others. I have ceased to participate. Is walking a participation? Or simply a movement through someone else's space?

I no longer care.

This heat has made me torpid.

In the hot noon I wander through the labyrinths of Cairo. Sir Thomas sleeps the deep sleep of the self-satisfied. My mind jerks about in my head, my eyes strain to feed it the images it craves. Some are stronger than others: the grimy pharmacies adorned with dried crocodile and stuffed baby elephants fill me with enough images for hours. On the raised floor of the shops sits the sleepy occupant, cross-legged, indifferent, and immune to his strange commerce. He smokes a drugged cigarette or a nargileh, as I have heard it called, which droops from his exquisite, sedated hand. I move beyond his blank staring eyes and am surrounded by the cries of the sellers of fruit, coffee and dates. A young boy runs past me shrieking the shout of the Sais or runner clearing the street for a carriage, which pursues him like a spurned wife. I am offered solace, treats for a man stupid enough to wander in the hot, midday sun, sherbets, lemonade or sweetmeats. But I want none of their wares and am curiously indifferent to my strange surrounds.

It is because, and it is hard for me to shape the words, I am lonely.

I do not know why I am here and I have no one to ask.

It is not just for the pictures or the statues or the history, it is for something else I cannot articulate. I am learning too much, yet I have learnt nothing. By nothing, I mean I am learning too much to generalise, and in this revelation I have been made aware of how often I used to express myself with the dogmatism of the ignorant. Now, my head has become too stuffed with images for any conclusions to be drawn about anything apart from one: namely, for some reason, mankind has felt impelled to make marks on surfaces other than themselves.

I do not, despite my immersion in some of the results, exactly know why. And I do not know why we, we being Sir Thomas and I, have to move so quickly through so many different places.

I find it difficult to recall the name of anyone I have met in the last month.

Today, however, I watched a woman at a well, and her still, calm face stilled me for a moment. She wore, like many of the women here, a dress of a loose blue shirt with long wide sleeves. Her slim wrists peered like snakes from the mouths of her elegant sleeves. When she moved, every movement jingled to the accompaniment of her silver bracelets. Her hands were tattooed with fine lines and curls. She scratched her chin and laughed and bit her lip. I would have loved to hold her hand and to trace the dusty lines of her face with my fingertips! To speak with her about her life here. To enter, somehow, into this environment that is as overwhelming as it is impenetrable.

But of course I could not.

I could not.

Her face was touched with a bluish tinge, her headdress decorated with piastres that hung like tiny moons over her eyes. These very same eyes held mine for a moment as she pulled her water towards her, and they were so gentle and good and merry I almost howled with sadness. But I did not. I looked down and when I looked up again she had forgotten me and was laughing with the children playing with pebbles at her feet. Then she moved away and was gone with her heavy load swaying and secure on her head.

A thousand things could have arrested my attention in that scene, but all, except her face, slipped away from me, more unreal than hallucinations. But she remained real and refused, for reasons I cannot begin to understand, to join in that dream pageant around her.

I decided to apply myself to drawing her gentle beauty, which in all truth would not have been displaced in a painting of the Madonna by Raffaele, but, as a result, was engulfed in a situation that only managed to confuse me further. For I at once was involved in something that baffled me, despite its apparent familiarity: I am a foreigner harassed in the marketplace. What happened was this: a menagerie of pompous ruffians emerged from nowhere and overwhelmed me. They banished at once my image of the well woman, in fact, momentarily exiled all of my senses, which were replaced with what I can only describe as terror. How could I not have noticed them before? Were they present when she was? Had I walked by them and not seen them? They were so vivid, my lack of awareness of them now seems to me as if they must have appeared from another world, another dimension, another dream. These splendid savages were clothed in the most magnificent and grubby finery, wild costumes of gorgeous scarlet and blue, framed with their long matted dark hair and sleepy dark complexions. They somehow managed to look at once makeshift and gloriously aristocratic. Noisy shopkeepers, stied in filth, called out to them with joy and respect, while strange and fearless half-naked children pulled at their silky legs. Long and vicious sabres, encased in red velvet scabbards, swung murderously on their thighs. They were more like wolves than any men I have ever seen, and all the more frightening in their astonishing resemblance to men. I tried to ignore them, hoping they would not be interested in such a pale and uninteresting specimen as myself, but when I took out my sketch book, all appeared to be forgotten except the wonder my drawing produced, and I was immediately surrounded, not only by these devils in human form, but what felt to me to be the entire population of the marketplace. How their deliciously villainous faces grinned and glowed and exhibited every variety of curiosity. Oh, such expression! Such heads! They closed in on me, and I found myself unable to breathe as easily as I should and so I stood and rapidly packed away my pad and pencils. I then attempted to push myself out of the melee, but they would have none of it and demanded

I continue to perform my foreign magic with my pencil. I pushed through them and began to run, but was followed by troops of boys and men, about fifty or sixty in number, all of them incomprehensibly shouting at me. I dived into all sorts of miserable alleys and back ways to avoid them but alas!

I might as well have tried to get rid of my own shadow. Finally, I finished up crouched and trembling in the corner of an alleyway slum, my hands held in front of me to ward them off, but as they approached, this terrible mob began to hoot and cry and pelt me with husks of corn. Suddenly, quite without my permission, a howl erupted from deep inside me, such a loud, terrifying howl I felt its terror myself, as if I were observing the workings of parts of my mind I had not before witnessed. It was as clever a piece of strategy as any I have initiated. I could have stopped them no more effectively if I had a battering ram and a private army. The mob stopped and was momentarily silent. The eyes looked at me and grew large, their jaws, as one, dropped to their chests. Then, they turned and fled, as if it were I who would murder them and not the other way around. All the while they shouted and wailed a strange Arabic song that faded into the cobblestones as they disappeared.

I did not mention this episode to Sir Thomas.

I Decide to Study the Egyptians

I must make something of this tiredness. I have a new rule: to read every evening before I retire. I will learn about the significance of these harsh places.

History will translate these mute rocks for me.

I have read that the earliest Bible writers were Egyptians, if not by birth, then by spirit and feeling. I read a simple sentence, Moses was found on the Nile.

Moses was found in the bulrushes of the Nile.

These words, read here, among places that are no longer arrangements of letters, take on an entirely different meaning. I realise, very strangely and very suddenly, what it is I am reading. We are headed to where Moses was found. He is not a story. He was found.

What I learnt as a child I must relearn as an adult. I must replace the story with the actual child, with Moses, who once was alive.

I am made acutely aware that since my childhood was replete with fiction, then the fiction must be transformed. The symbolic language of the Egyptians stained every particle of dust. The stardust, the moon dust, the earth dust. Everything written in the air, clearly, for everyone to read.

In England I remember the way I looked at the sky. My head would lean back and my face would turn in the right direction, but I would see nothing but a mess of light and stars, indeterminate constellations whose only function was to illuminate the sky and furnish my imagination with props for paintings. My lack of system, my lack of harmony, my sheer ignorance of what our canopy is composed of, has begun to disgust me. I must wheel the constellations into a line in my mind, create order out of abstractions and learn to understand the exact laws of Divine Creation. However, I will try not to be misled by mysteries.

But the sun and the moon and the stars are above me now and demand I take notice of their power.

The Lebanese Mountains

We have left the cities behind and entered the wilderness.

We travel hard and immensely fast, rising at dawn and riding for eight to ten hours a day. I feel keenly the loss of opportunity for the improvement of my sketches. By the time we reach camp, there is usually very little daylight left in which to do anything but eat and collapse in exhaustion. I try to remember, as I lie with my tired limbs under the stars or in tents or the strange, hospitable home of occasional sheikhs, the places and people I have seen, to burn them into my memory, to place them there like a drawing in a drawer, so that I will be able, if need be, to pull them out and consult them.

The poor, blighted animals that carry us, either horses or mules, are almost always in a sorry state, and I feel their misery deep in my bones. The sand and heat and sheer mileage we have covered have forced these animals to occasionally drop from beneath us without warning.

I have been thrown or fallen and been injured so many times now, I have lost count of my damage, and refuse to acknowledge or look at my cuts or bruises. I have been thrown into streams and down small embankments, but cannot punish the miserable beast whose job it is to carry me: after all, no doubt I would toss them off in the first instance if I were forced to carry them. But at least, for the first time in my life, I am almost a decent horseman. I have begun to anticipate the animal's intention before it has had time to think it. I feel my kinship with these beasts. I will not beat them.

I wear a fez tied with two handkerchiefs, one white, the other red. I have grown a beard and moustachio, and wear a pair of large boots of Russian leather that are so soft and pliable I can shake them off and on with ease. I wear them outside my trousers. They reach halfway up my legs. My upper body is adorned with a white blouse that flaps in a satisfying way in the wind.

I would give anything for my family to appear and for them to witness their brother and son dressed like a wild and romantic vagrant. Sir Thomas gains much enjoyment from my appearance, as I do from his. He looks like a plum pudding dressed as a young boy. Is he stouter, or have his clothes grown smaller? I sometimes cannot look at him, for fear of flinging myself off my mount in laughter. But he would be even funnier if he were not so dreadfully stuffed full of himself. I am obliged to pull my scarves low over my ears, in a vain attempt to stem the sound of his self-mythologizing. I long for blinkers to block the failed images of men who cluster around him every time we stop. To witness the value of my companion's title is to witness human sycophancy at its most vile. Grown men simper and oil around him as if he were a maharajah, and how he laps it up! The world, to Sir Thomas, is a place built of cream, and he is an appalling, corpulent cat.

Witnessing the genuflection such idiocy demands makes me very tired of our planet. I have seen so much disgusting selfishness since I have left England that I am in danger of becoming a misanthrope. But the places we have seen! And having to tolerate the company of Sir Thomas has been worth the visions granted to me. They distract my mind so intensely, that I can forget, if only for a moment, who is at my side. Pinara, for example. What a most extraordinary place! A place where men are turned into midgets by the sheer scale of their environment. The atmosphere of unseen presences in this place is almost overwhelming. The wind hits the cliffs with a dreadful hissing moan. The sun beats the earth and stone to no avail: nothing will crumble them.

Gods must coexist uneasily with devils in the crevasses, but despite their proximity neither would be able to find each other in the day or night, but in their dreams must eavesdrop on each other's breathing. The rocks, many hundreds of feet high, tower above the city and their faces are pitted with the infection of a thousand excavations. And nothing, despite their defilement, can compare to the tombs these history thieves have revealed.

From the citadel of Hos we enjoy a view of eternity by the morning sunlight; and as we stand in the ruins of a Roman building, so quickly do our bodies shrink into the dust of time, we fancy ourselves turned into Romans; I admit without compunction that such beauty (although the word is too small) has made me too romantic to be a good companion to myself.

We pass shepherds tending goats, who live in black, camel hair tents, surrounded with staring naked children. We meet one hundred and fifty camels on their way to Smyrna. Their bells clang and tinkle and the drivers are as gay and as bright as colours could ever be. It is difficult to reconcile myself to the idea that here before me are real men, not players in a wondrous circus, or the employees of a giant mechanical doll company. These men can bleed and weep and love! But still, despite their very real flesh, they are as insubstantial as the feathers of exotic parrots.

The wild plains and vast and snowy mountain peaks are exquisitely beautiful, too beautiful almost to look at, as if looking with such impoverished eyes might defile such splendour. When they first appeared, I nearly leapt from my skin. Had I died, and been flung into heaven?

The Inability to Speak

Richard, look!

We have been riding for hours. I am exhausted. I can no longer focus on anything but my hands and the small, curved ears of my pony.

I look up but am blinded by the vibrations of my own tiredness.

I turn to Sir Thomas.

What would you like me to look at?

Over there, Richard. It is really quite wonderful.

He stands in his stirrups and points to a distant peak.

I peer but cannot see anything.

Surely you can see it, Richard?

What?

I do not know how to tell him what it is I cannot see.

I canter away from him and hear his voice fade from my sphere.

I am covered in dust.

Myths

Sir Thomas has lent me his book of the stories of Egyptian mythology. Horus and Seth were brothers, who engaged in a violent conflict. In this they bear an uncanny resemblance to Cain and Abel. This I find curious. In their fight Horus lost an eye and Seth a testicle but the god Thoth intervened on behalf of Horus, and the stolen eye was restored to its owner. After gaining possession of it, Horus presented it to his father, King Osiris. His eye was meant to protect the king against Seth's violence. But to no avail. Osiris was slain by Seth's madness. In terrible grief the sister and wife of Osiris, Isis, and his brother Nephthys searched for their brother. They found him dead.

The thought of finding the body of a sibling quickens and tears at the deepest parts of my heart. If moving through the world is to prepare oneself for some future, unknown grief, then such an image, a concrete image of horror, but built from the flesh of familiar faces is almost too hard to bear.

The imagination is the greatest assassin and the cruellest image giver of all.

Nonetheless, the absurdity of my situation is never lost to me, quite despite the seriousness of what has been revealed. This rotund, short-sighted tea sipper is responsible for my introduction to Osiris. He has placed my hand in his, and his in mine. He has pulled my head close to his in order to hear his words all the more clearly.

Sir Thomas, unwitting medium, socialite to the stars, deaf man, blind man, unbeliever.

O Heaven speaks, earth trembles. Thou shalt not be cut up, Osiris.

These are stories written to plague dreams.

Speed

We travel too far and too fast for me to sketch. As a result, I am not working hard enough and the thought of such lost opportunity torments me. I must resort to making mental sketches, but sometimes my fury at my idle hands blots them with darkness. We ride so hard, and often through such filth and inconvenience, it is impossible to see around me the things that lie beneath such an infernal rocky country that grows nothing but large stones. Consumed with such a mood, I reach for my history in vain but see nothing but stones. No stories. Simply a brutal, incomprehensible surface.

I may as well be crossing the moon, for all its mysterious connection to who I am.

When this happens, I cannot speak to anyone.

But now I am awake, or rather have been forced to see beyond my own narrow expectations. We have passed through the wild passes of Engadi by moonlight, and I have been shaken to my core, so that I can feel the movement of every drop of blood through my veins and feel every sliver of bone in me shiver. This place looks to my eyes (my diseased eyes) like the end of the world, but what a finale it is! Extinct craters of volcanoes plunge into the bowels around us, and some of the mountains bend into the most extravagant shapes. The wind howls without a mouth, and the moon beats the earth like a slave driver. No birds but prehistoric ones. No animals but snakes and lizards that become the colour of rocks or sand at will.

All of them shout at me to conceive of the possibility of shape and substance in the world, shape and substance that gives the sound of the gods a form. Yes, I will open my mind, I tell the moonlight, and my mind will flourish, because the soil in which it is growing is uncommonly good.

But I cannot reduce the response of my soul to mere words.

This is a response that demands two things of me: action and pictures.

I Read

I read what I have been told is the earliest expression in literature of a belief in life after death.

I read: Recitation: Atum, this Osiris is thy son; thou hast caused him to flourish and live. He lives, this king lives; he is not dead, this King is not dead. He has not perished, this King has not perished. If he does not endure, this King does not endure. He endures, this King endures. I do not understand these words. But they stick in my head like a bee in honey.

Another Letter from Home

Maria writes me a sad letter and speaks of how she lacks my presence. She tells me how all of my family are lacking me, but I do not believe her. How can they miss what they no longer know?

I search my heart for charity, and find it crouched in a corner of my heart.

I find it in the fact that they do not know that they no longer know me.

She tells me that father speaks of me often; all of my family do, about what it is I could possibly be seeing, or thinking or doing. She writes that when she thinks of the drawings and sketches I will bring home, she can hardly contain her excitement and can only dream of what I am seeing.

See well, she says, and remember everything.

That, I think, is too much of a task for anyone.

She tells me God will keep me well, because He is our God and loves us and we are good and worthy of care.

I do not know whether what she says still holds true.

She wonders if I have seen the Pyramids and the Great Sphinx. She says she does not know where I am now, as my letters reach my family from such a long away. My letters make her sad, she says, because they remind her, in such a tangible way, that I am somewhere else.

I wish I could tell her where it is I have come to. Some days I do not know myself.

Maria does not believe I am telling her everything, and reminds me to share my thoughts with her. My thoughts, she informs me, are more precious to her than any ancient relic.

She does not want her brother to drown or become lost or set upon by brigands.

In London, apparently, nothing is changed. It is colder and the nights longer. The fogs have begun. She has a new coat but little energy.

There is much to be seen from our front window, but my sisters who chide her for inaction berate her.

The boys are growing and shout so. Father rarely seems to find time to stay at home.

If I was there, she tells me, she should not lack me.

She orders me again to see well and to draw beautiful pictures, and to speed home to my loving family, but especially to see my loving sister, Maria.

My Head Is a House

I have come to the realisation that there are at least two versions of me travelling with Sir Thomas, each as imaginary and as real as the life inside a painting. Living inside my head is like dwelling in a serene and well-run household, that unfortunately has built into its foundations a few haunted rooms that guests should, at all costs, be discouraged from entering.

Imagine.

Sometimes I am in a calm antechamber eating a sunny breakfast when the sound of music will abruptly begin in a room I cannot locate.

Perhaps a piano trio, perhaps a persistent triangle, perhaps the clapping of an intimate audience, who, for some reason, have been issued tickets to be entertained by the deep recesses of their host's mind.

And where is the host to be found? Wandering the lonely corridors, no doubt, looking for a way in. Or a way out.

I can only recognise myself if I look away from who I expect myself to be, a feeling not unlike when as a boy I would search for a particular star and father would say, look away, Richard, from the place in the sky you think it to be. You will see it out of the corner of your eye.

And I would.

If I avoid myself at all costs, I might, for a few hours, remain calm.

But.

I find myself gazing at sand and seeing green hills.

I notice hideous faces glaring at me from the faces of sweet young girls.

I see the silhouette of a pig in the mild eyes of a camel.

I lie stuck to my bed, covered in sweat as the mattress breathes and groans beneath me.

I have forgotten the names of my own sisters and my own brothers.

I speak happily, for hours, with my dead mother, whose hand I feel stroke mine, and curse the breath of my father, who is revealed to me as an impostor of the highest order.

I walk in sunlight and feel the hot glare of the moon burn my skin.

I see scorpions the size of men haunting ruins.

I crash into walls I do not see. I pluck poisonous flowers and dream I boil them for tea. I spend hours polishing teaspoons I do not need.

I long to dilute my colours with mirages, to make them hot and trembling.

Osiris

I read that Osiris has his helpers and messengers, who execute his command. Apparently these helpers may be objects of terror. This terror is perhaps accounted for by the fact that after being slain by his own son, he became a ruler of the kingdom of the dead, the underworld. He rightly threatens those who have sinned against him and whom he condemns as a judge. He is served by demons. They are his executioners.

Osiris is to be dreaded, despite the fact that it was he who was wronged by his child.

Perhaps it is a father's wrath that lends his anger such validity.

The world is accustomed to the wrath of fathers. Or, in the case of Christianity, the indifference of the Father who allowed his only son to be murdered.

But Osiris is also a man who has become a god and risen from the dead, and speaks clearly with the moon, which rises every night as he did after he was slain.

Osiris had parents, Nut and Geb. But it was his own son who slew him, who made him a god through his act of violence.

And yet, I do not understand; Osiris would never have become a god if his son had not slain him. But why should a son slay a father? Why should a father be slain to make him a god? He was a man, then a hero, then a god. He has been, perhaps is, every man.

Where is the right and wrong in all of this? Who is right and wrong?

The Solace of Some Words, the Difficulty of Others

When I read, my sense of disorientation and my fear of instability pass. There is something in these histories that soothes me, challenges me, pulls me up out of chaos and into order. The order of truths that have lasted, dug deep into stones. I lie in a dark cool room and detach myself from such fancies. I say to myself again and again, no. I imagine in my hot head an artist who has taken too much laudanum. I think of this artist inside me, and order him off the premises.

Sometimes it works. Sometimes it doesn't.

And sometimes I am so fascinated by the images this artist conjures for me, I do not want him to leave.

Sir Thomas, to whom I have only given the slightest intimation of my troubles, has, for once, been reassuring in the banality of his advice and observations. He has told me of many men who have become light-headed with the heat.

Sir Thomas, light-headed? I would describe this more as heavy-headed, lump-headed, dream-headed, horror-headed, and wrong-headed. I am almost shrill. I hear myself from a long way off, as if I was someone else, an eavesdropper listening to me.

He laughs long and loud, and I will put it down to my illness that I detected a note of hysteria in his laughter.

Richard, Richard. I warned you of the sun. It is a powerful drug. Your mind will accustom itself, I promise you. You must drink more boiled water, more tea. You must not, on any account, let yourself become dehydrated.

He tells me my illness has been caused, apparently, by a lack of water in the body. But while I have been drinking copious amounts of tea, to counteract my thirst and the apparent aridity of my interior, it has not helped me so much as made me uncomfortably bloated.

It is difficult to locate cause and effect in all of this.

Imp whispers to me ceaselessly, who is qualified to say who is sun-struck? How can something so golden, so soft, so elusive cause such harm?

The sun hammers away at my head like an argumentative lover. I curse it, wrestle with it, and, during moments of respite, soak its light deep into my bones, into my skin, my veins.

But for all its cruelty, I do not want it to leave me.

Buried Among the Ruins of Solitary Limbs

In ancient Syria, buried among the ruins of solitary limbs, I find a pottery shard.

I hold it to my cheek to visualise it all the better. The earth has delivered it to me, indeed almost tripped me up with its gift, and I would, at all costs, respect such an offering, to find ways of appreciating the earth's generosity. I look at it from all angles and consider how best to appreciate it.

A useless thing, a pottery shard, except as an aide-memoire for a memory I have never had. To think, however, of the brown hands that spun such a simple thing from clay, and placed it in a fire and then filled it with wine or milk or honey, is to breathe a little life into these ransacked and abandoned temples, to glimpse the lives of individuals threaded into a grand narrative like cotton into a carpet.

I sit in the shade of a ruined wall, and ignore Sir Thomas' cries as he searches for me, and let the clay whisper to me. I hold it close to my ears.

It smells of dust and sunlight and faintly of piss. It is too disappointing.

I cannot, however hard I breathe, smell the wine or the honey or the milk.

I have read: death is simply a phase of tiredness from which it is likely you will awake more refreshed than you ever were. Some Egyptians believed this. Some also believed that blood restores life to the dead. All dead, or all alive, who held it before me?

Hardship in Palestine

It is too dry, too cruel, too unfriendly here. Both my skin and that of Sir Thomas is as cracked as a riverbed deprived of rain.

I was, for a week, too ill to speak, wracked with the dreadful emptying of my body and a constant thirst that could never be slaked. Our rooms were filthy, the housekeeper slatternly. Sir Thomas and I could hardly speak to each other, so depressed were we with our situation.

But I continued to read, when my head had cooled a little, and when my eyes ceased to burn and distort the world it is their job to inform me of. I read how god is magic reflected in the blazing sun. I read that the fruit of the god suits the soil of the living. I have read that we are reminded of cosmic renewal every time we witness the Lord of the West, our sun, sinking before night.

I have come to believe that man must accomplish the work of revelation for himself.

When I could finally walk we ventured into the streets only to be confronted with the slaughter of a dog on the street. Men chatted casually as they hacked at it and for a few seconds it shrieked horribly. Even women and children walked by without giving the poor beast so much as a glance. Finally, its astonished, slow-blinking eyes gave the only indication that it still lived, and then, passing quickly to somewhere else, it died.

The sight forced me back to my room for a few more days.

I am too foreign here even for myself. I see no point in being here, none whatsoever. Sir Thomas readily agrees, despite his mania for adventure. He promises we shall leave as soon as I am strong enough to travel. He has a friend with a barge on the Nile, or so he says. One we can drift on, and be waited upon. It is the first time I have heard him say something that has inspired affection in my soul for him.

We Float Together, in Light

I have never lived in such opulence as this, on the barge of a diplomat, on the Nile, the silent Nile.

I amuse myself play-acting. I am Anthony or Hadrian.

But not Osiris. Perhaps I will kneel before him. It is growing in me, the urge to do so. He guards the other world, the one into which we will all eventually pass. It is important to give him his due. I am in his country, on his river, where his own son or brother cast him.

I search the brown water hungrily for traces of his remains, but there is nothing to be seen beneath such an inscrutable surface. Only the counterpoint of drifting, dying, hovering insects. As I look, I am niggled by a paradox: if Osiris is a god to these people, and one to whom the river was his blood, then how can he, in fact, drown in himself?

It is a feeling, however, if not an actuality, I know well.

I read: he swims or floats under thee.

I look and look for him while the Nubian crew slay indifferent chickens for supper and we drift past picturesque hamlets.

I read: death by drowning was blessed by the ancient Egyptians, because it mirrored the death of Osiris.

I read: in the trial that was held in the heavens after the foul murder of Osiris, Osiris is granted eternal life, a vast kingdom, heaven and earth, and the fields of Iaru, the Horite villages, the Sethite villages, the cities and the Nomes.

Osiris has become the river, and his son Seth, who slew him, the desert. Nothing grows from Seth. Everything green springs from the bounty of Osiris.

I read: he rode in a barque called the great ship of Eternity and Everlasting.

His wife and sister Isis and his brother Nephthys became his attendant falcons. These birds are the symbols of mourning. Sometimes Isis is a swallow.

Swallows here fly thick and fast around the helm at twilight. They sometimes resemble bats, or thin, exquisite girls, diving through air. I go ashore and walk through bean and Doura fields beneath the crazed and courtly antics of crested larks and spurwinged plovers. Geese and ducks are plentiful. On sand banks large flocks of cranes perch on the rigging or awning rails. Every cluster of mud huts honours the pigeons. It is customary to place large earthenware jars with protruding branches outside homes for the birds to sit on.

The villages look like deserted ant hills. Conglomerations of rubbish huddle around their extremities, almost lost among the occasional belt of palms that surrounds them. Coloured plates and saucers hang from the doors to avert the gaze of the evil eye.

This is a hopeful land, a place for birds to land.

I read: The bird comes, the birds come; this is Isis with Nephthys. They have come seeking their brother Osiris.

There are truths preserved in the places they pass: recorded upon pyramids, tombs, temples, triumphant arches, statuary and churches. I look for him in the river and in the places he passed.

And I look up into the sky, where his soul became a star and see the birds circle wide and flaming around me before disappearing into His bright eye.

The monotonous, soothing desert nags my concentration. I do not like to step on Seth, who killed his father.

He disappears eventually, fades into another region, and Osiris reigns supreme. Dust and dry sand has given way to plump green trees, to shade, to laboriously worked areas where seeds might grow to adulthood before suffocation. Deserted estuaries and sand bars, meeting places for fish and birds, emerge before us like slow loops. Sometimes the river splits in two and curves around an island thick with fig trees and exhausted palms. Sometimes we float past villages where listless eyes widen at the sight of the glitter of our barge, its polish, its quiet, its lack of any function but pleasure.

I am glutted on light. Light above me, light below me, we are floating through Egypt on light.

My limbs cannot believe their lassitude, but in truth luxuriate in such inactivity after months of backbreaking, swift travel. To move through a place with such little effort, I am not sure I deserve this.

But I will earn it.

This barge is even aglow at night, when the sky is black and thick with pinpricks.

Orion shines on us. I read: Orion is Osiris' star.

There is a chandelier in the dining room, which sways and glitters with each gentle wave. Red lights dance off the silver, reflecting the blood-red cushions. Blue lights scatter in the face of fluttering silk. Yellow light refracts into silver goblets from the moon.

This is not a place for our English God. He would be blinded by such brightness. He would cough into his clergyman's collar and sip his tea with averted eyes.

This place is someone else's domain, someone I haven't yet met.

We are treated like princes, surrounded by servants as smooth as snakes, who wear white gloves and stare blankly from hot eyes that will not look into mine. Sir Thomas and I have become actors in a theatrical troupe whose speciality is the reenactment of ancient luxury. We pretend we are accustomed to such extravagance. I, at least, am not. My masquerade forces a hilarity from me, that has a tendency to land in chilled soup. Sir Thomas chides me, with a tired voice.

Do not laugh so, Richard, they will think you mock them.

I mock no one but unbelievers, Sir Thomas, I reply, then stifle my laughter again.

Sir Thomas, I continue, what do you believe in?

Poor Sir Thomas looks at me, sighs, continues drinking his soup and starts to read the book he has so pointedly propped up against the salt canister.

I do believe he would hire a translator and hang the expense if only he could find one that spoke my language.

I drink my soup and attempt to remain quiet, but find it hard to suppress the feelings that continuously erupt from me.

Our beds are enormous and covered in silk mosaic. The night air is fresh and cool with flower blooms. The air sucks dry any attempt at conversation. At night we anchor, as the waters are too perilous with sand banks to continue our journey in the dark. Apparently no one can see the danger that lurks beneath the black water. No one.

Some of the servants sit around a small fire on the shore, guarding us from bandits or beasts. Which is it? Who knows? No one tells us, no one speaks frankly to us.

I long for a fellow human being to look me in the face, as an equal. Here I am above or below. It is lonely.

My family have become as faint to me as apparitions. They are my blood, but even bloodstains fade.

The sound of laughing servants mocks the lack of joy between Sir Thomas and myself. I will no longer speak about nothing with him. My life is too short for such exchanges. I watch the dark river and wonder about what lies beyond it.

Warmed by the light of Orion.

Invisible dogs make the nights hideous with their howls.

In the mornings swimming children paddle near our barge and beg baksheesh from us. Others flick switches and drive indolent buffalo towards the water to drink. Some attempt to come aboard but our servants swiftly expel them. I saw a small brown hand clutch the railing I have clutched so many times, and then witnessed a servant, supposedly in our employ, hit that same small hand with a stick. The hand disappeared but happily not the child, who swam howling to the shore.

Women wash clothes on the riverbank with the restraint of moths. These women are such that the Masters would gladly have used them for models. They disorientate me. They make me forget whether I am in a picture or observing one. It is not an altogether unpleasant disorientation.

Camels mumble deep into the water. Trees bend their lovely arms towards us, across the river's broad back.

Sir Thomas is almost always writing but has adopted a new, irritating habit. He drums and rolls his fingertips on tables or his thighs when he writes, and the sound is amplified in my head until I must beg him to stop. But as I am now apparently officially ill, he excuses my irritability and tries to talk to me in the soothing tones of an ancient nanny talking to the idiot offspring of a suburban doctor.

I turn from him in disgust. Poor Sir Thomas. My indifferent attempts to communicate with him have become as transparent, as feeble as the wings of a dying mosquito.

Where Do Pictures Go if They Are Not Born?

We drift down this eternal river as if it will never reach the sea, which has become something as unimaginable as cool skin or walking on the moon.

My hands are as listless as my mind is overextended. I cannot draw.

A pencil would be far too heavy for the frailty that permeates every inch of my poor fingers, those narrow brown things that dangle from my palms and have such import in the translation of the images in my mind.

I wonder what I would do if I were to lose them. If some devil were to sever them and toss them away. Would my toes adapt to holding the brush? My mouth? Would I become a writer in images, a madman? But what would happen to all of the images imprisoned in my mind? Where would they go? Would people be able to see stories in my eyes? The world must be full of the ghosts of restless, unborn pictures, the ones that lived in dreams and eyes but were never realised in their material form. The very air must be a museum to such frustration. I have tried to grab the invisible shapes that crowd my head and wonder if I could hold in my head and heart the images born of artists long dead? Could my body become the conduit for their aborted visions? And what of such an eventuality in reverse? Could another artist paint the pictures that live on only in my head and not on my canvas? In case of such an eventuality, I am insisting of my memory that it become the artist. It must paint the pictures in the air, and claim authorship at once. I will not be thieved by spirits. I am resolute on this.

Almost Christmas

It is almost Christmas, but sand and water have supplanted the snow of Sussex Street.

But what water this is, water that changes its mind and colour at every river bend.

What is it? A home for birds or people? A drink for a thirsty field?

A black line built to dissect sand?

It is an infinite story that refuses to reveal its purpose.

I do not recall such complex rivers at home.

My brothers and sisters would have chosen their tree by now and would have become once again accustomed to the fog and damp of a London winter.

I have not heard a word from them for so long I struggle to recall the features of their faces, which I know, as they are young, will have already changed. The feelings they engender in me are solid, but in the way a mud hut that is too wet is solid. Their details are becoming lost to me.

I weep when I think of their sweetness. They are too good for their brother Richard who has become so full of images he cannot draw a single picture.

I am tormented with loneliness.

We Go Ashore

Our boat is docked at Siut, and we go ashore to visit the bazaar.

I wander away from Sir Thomas and revel in the lack of his proximity. There are wonderful things on offer here. Carpets, shawls and draperies of every colour and cloth, stagnant perfumes in strangely shaped and tinted bottles, the vermilion and primrose of countless Turkish slippers, local pottery, covered in wild red and black patterns. I would bet that anything could be bought here; I have spied second-rate German cigars, spectacles from Paris and cloth from Manchester. The distance these objects have covered!

It is enough to boggle the mind.

Turks in light dresses and large white turbans stroll about like sedate statues while Bedouin Arabs as dignified as gods canter down the narrow streets on delicate ponies.

I am filled with a wild desire. I wish I had been born a blackguard, a robbing mountaineer, or a minstrel, so I could escape into the hills and live a life more adventurous than the one that awaits me on my return. I could have a wife with golden piastres on her forehead. I would live with her in a small hut, filled with rugs and jewels, and she would love me, and never speak. We would never learn each other's language.

We would speak only with eyes and touch.

She would collect water from a well, and every day I would witness it.

Her silence would be her wedding gift to me.

Mine to her would be my protection, and my love.

My future stretches before me and the thought of it does not fill me with anything even approaching the emotions that the wild sounds of the tabor inspire in my soul.

I let music wash through me until I am suffused with a blissful delirium. I find a step on which to sit and sketch. For once no one takes notice of me. My hands fly over the page and images appear both before me and beneath my hand: the strange dress of street musicians, the bubbling water fountain in the middle of this delicious square, the generous trees, the dazzling dresses of sloe-eyed women, the stately dance of camels.

I lay my reason before this place. I give it my gift of line.

If only I had a friend who could hold me tight. These feelings are too big in me, too big for my body. Thoughts are generated in me I do not understand.

I hold my face to the sky and the heat makes me happy.

The Sun

The sun bounces off the stone on the riverbank. It forms balls of light that spin and surprise as they race and leap towards me.

I read that in many Ancient languages, the meaning of the eye and the meaning of the sun are expressed in the same word.

I read that the sun was named Osiris; giver of life, bestower of blessings, just judge, blessed and condemned, inspector, moderator, star guider, soul of the world, governor of nature.

I read that Osiris is described as the son of man.

How many sons of men can exist on earth? Men give birth to men and men then kill men.

It is endless, although being simply a son of one man has begun to feel equally bewildering.

I look from my eye and penetrate the sun with my gaze. My eyes, my own two suns.

The suns of one man.

This sun, of course, is yellow, as light tends to be, yellow and white but filled with other colour as well. Colour I could only describe with crude approximation if you were to ask, but colour nonetheless, and it is the colour of this world and the other one, for which I do not yet have a name. Perhaps it is mainly blue. Perhaps it was born in tones of brown, or even a cornflower, an iris, a sunflower, a child's bright ball.

When Maria was a child, my father asked her, Maria, what is your favourite colour, and without hesitation, she answered: rainbow.

A sun-kissed branch. A bleached shard of bone. The golden heart of a daisy, dressed in its white skirt. It bounces back and forth, so full of rhythm and light, it makes me laugh.

I had never before noticed how well our largest star dances for us.

Sir Thomas repeats like an old bore, his voice rising with every syllable, Richard, you are sun-struck, you must stay indoors. I must insist that you not sit in this glare, in this heat.

I ignore his bumblings and hold my face up to the sky.

Struck by the sun. Such an idea, a fist of heat. Sir Thomas cannot recognise his own poetry.

A delightful, clean hammer. A glorious fate. A blade of light, softened with mezzotint. As good, and as versatile, as a knife that can slice butter and cut loose a noose.

Occasionally, I hide the joy of my discovery from him and surrender, falsely, to his solicitude.

Cool towels on my forehead, and my cabin is dark even in daylight.

A boy with evasive eyes brings me tea, weak with lemon and too much sugar. Wafers, cold soup, dry bread. Occasionally a fig, but only if Sir Thomas believes my nerves are up to accommodating its sweetness. I chew voraciously. In truth, I have never felt better.

Banishing Sunlight

I agree, with a voice so full of deceit I am astonished the world does not toss me overboard, with Sir Thomas' refusal to allow that which I most welcome into my domain. He comes into my cabin, uninvited and banishes the sunlight with a lumbering hand. He inspires a silence in me, a tightness in my heart despite his generosity. He is too easy to watch. He leaves himself as open as a discarded novel, but quite despite his incessant commentary, cannot see a thing. He is so rarely aware of what is actually happening around him, I wonder at his thirst for travel. He is a man who believes himself so literate with the visual world, but I do not believe he has ever looked at his own shadow.

Sir Thomas, I resist shouting, without looking down, describe the colour of your shirt.

I would bet my boots he could not. He is not a man, for all his travelling, who ever looks.

He is round and full of himself, not unlike the sun, but definitely darker for all his cheer. I am, it is said, indebted to him, and with this I do not quarrel. He has brought me here, and quite despite himself, has revealed this place to me.

It is time now to leave. We begin our slow trail home. Home. It has become a curious word to me.

The Return

We travel back to England, the boat arguing with waves, ceaselessly groaning with the effort of its passage.

The air is already cold, the sky more brittle, the food more foul and familiar in its foulness.

I refuse to sleep in a cabin with Sir Thomas, and he has, so far, resisted persuading me otherwise.

When I am not keeping watch over my travelling companion, I wander the decks examining the heavens and reassuring stars. The moon slides slowly beneath clouds and mesmerises me. When not walking, I sit still and watch the light on the ocean, drinking ale after ale to keep me awake. Occasionally fish leap high above the water, and then, in a flash of silver, disappear beneath the glittering surface of their world. Is the world smaller or bigger if observed through the eye of a fish? Is size dependent on the viewer or what is being viewed?

I do not know.

My mind's eye is preoccupied with things not human, and my heart is full of terrible knowledge.

I am certain. However far-fetched it may sound, Sir Thomas, despite his innocuous appearance, is wrong in every decision he has ever made.

I observe him, and wish, no, long for the possibility that what I have seen in his company is simply a story that could be flung aside. What a blessing that would be. If only simple stories surrounded me.

But nothing I have seen or learnt is a story. They are ideas as tough and tangible as skulls.

A steward interrupts my watch with a falsely solicitous smile.

I grip my hands in my lap. I am so disgusted by this man's simpering manner I can hardly look at him.

I shout at him, bring me more ale. I must speak loudly to such fools so they can hear me.

They would not know the difference between a murder and an act of kindness.

They would not know what they had been given if pearls were poured on their eyelids.

The steward is too stupid to understand my communication, and looks at me so strangely it takes all of my willpower not to throttle him for his impudent staring eyes. But I know, if I am to make headway, that I must learn to be more generous, more subtle than this. He does not know in what danger he has placed himself by working on board such a vessel, one whose cargo of flesh is so thoroughly rotten.

He scuttles off on his foolish, indignant legs, and I resume my watchfulness.

The moon has nudged itself closer to its destination.

My ale is brought to me, with a sniff and a stiff back.

It tastes of salt.

I wish that I could swallow stars that would shoot me into the sky and let me float above all of this, but I cannot, and so have no choice in the matter.

However flimsy the attempt, I must try to protect whatever innocence there may be on board this vessel. Perhaps there is a child asleep somewhere. God forbid. A child on such a boat is like a piece of steak before a starving man. Who will protect that child if I do not keep watch?

Sir Thomas sits, laughing comfortably, with others who must be equally corrupt or doubly stupid. He brazenly shuffles and spreads his cards as he smokes and drinks and allows his eyes to roll around his head without settling once, with honesty, on anything. He will no longer look at me. Perhaps there is hope for the man, as he is so obviously satiated with his own guilt. He drinks like someone in a desert. He smokes like a sickened chimney. He is so glad to be with his fellowmen, these men who would travel with him into the depths of innocent souls to see how much they could borrow for their soul-coffers.

He does not know how much I know.

He would frighten himself if he did.

He must not win this game.

I would warn the captain if I could, but sly Sir Thomas has warned him first, I can see it in the kindly glances he throws in my direction, as if I were a stray who begged to taste an occasional scrap of humanity. He still calls me sun-struck, but less constantly, and with, I think, less solicitousness.

The Captain believes Sir Thomas, he believes in his title and his egg-shell authority, he believes in his corpulence and his obese vowels and his plump, determined hands.

Poor Captain. He has no awareness of the danger into which he has placed himself by playing cards with Sir

Thomas. They pretend the stakes are nothing more than a round of drinks. It is quite possible that Sir Thomas will drag the ship under with him on his way home into the bowels of the earth.

Destroying the Mark of the Devil

I cannot help the lifting of my hand when Sir Thomas deals the cards. And I cannot help but feel the heat that touches my hand when it comes into contact with my forehead. And I cannot help it if I must then go to the looking glass to see what has caused such heat to come from my forehead. And should I not be then applauded for cutting away from my forehead what the devil has placed there?

He marked me at birth for observance and now the mark is gone.

I will not bear Sir Thomas' revulsion at the blood that pours from my skin. It is only blood, which is no less natural than air, and we walk through air every moment of our lives.

But of course Sir Thomas is repulsed. I have cut away the birthmark with which the devil insisted on burning me when he fought against my arrival in the world.

My heart is happy, even if I know it is a brief happiness. I cannot feel my wound, because it is not, despite the blood, a wound.

It is a shield.

The agents of Sir Thomas will have a harder time recognising me now.

The respite will be momentary, as I am perfectly aware that they will find a way of marking me again, but when that happens I will cut that mark away from me as well.

At least I have stopped them playing cards.

The Captain, and any child on board, is safe now, if only for a while. Until we arrive, when they, like me, will be on their own.

Paris

The last stage of our travels.

It is only a relatively short journey home now, but I have become incapable of imagining what that destination means.

Is it somewhere I have come from, or somewhere I must now create?

It is all I can do to contain my fury without distraction, and if injury is to be prevented of someone whose name I cannot bring myself to utter, think of, or write, then I must leave. Without farewell. Without thanks, which would choke my throat with bile.

I am stuffed full of him. I cannot have another morsel of his presence, however small the bite.

For him to suggest, and in the most veiled and falsely solicitous terms, that I am unwell, that my mind has become unbalanced and overstimulated and that it should, forthwith, be seen to, that it is, in a word, me, who needs immediate expert care, would be laughable if it were not so wholly tragic that the world has become so skewed about who is, and who is not, of sound mind. For a man so ignorant, so pompous, so full of his own fictitious worth to tell me, in no uncertain terms, that he is better, healthier, and more able to navigate his way through the purely superficial realm he likes to call the present I cannot stomach. And so I will never see him again. Because if I were to see him, even for a moment, I would have to remove him from this world, because it is men like him who make this planet a darker, more dishonest, more corrupt place.

Our views are at such variance, it seems astonishing that we share the same human shape. He makes no allowances for me as I, time and again, have made for him.

Of course, he will feel injured, and believe himself unthanked for his generosity.

I would like an appropriate response to this hypocrisy burnt into his brain. It is not generosity that makes a man like him drag a man like me halfway around the world. No, it is simply a less obvious form of selfishness and egotism than that which a more honest man would more plainly state. This man's selfishness is actually more corrupt than its less subtle manifestations. I ask, is it generous for a man to demand sycophantic praise? To demand thanks for something that will make no mark whatsoever on his wealth, but will inflate his supposed reputation for artistic philanthropy? To demand from others conversation that will simply serve to bolster his own non-existent or borrowed opinions?

No, I will say it again, and again, shout if I have to. He is not generous. These are not actions for which any vaguely sane or sensitive person would be thankful.

He has done nothing but enraged me. The rage that grows from the realisation that all that is apparent is not necessarily written on the surface of things. But perhaps, on reflection, I should thank Sir Thomas for one thing; namely, he has cleared the clutter of sentimentality from my heart as surely as if he had taken a broom to my soul.

I will return to London immediately and discover the truth.

It should not be difficult to find, to recognise.

I, the neophyte, shall see it written in the skies of heaven's face.

Arrival London, 1843

I ring the doorbell, a deep, soft sound that ricochets through the house.

I hear its journey finishing deep in the kitchen, rattling the pots, where it rests.

The parlour windows are curtained thick and close against the night air.

A sliver of light allows only a tantalising glimpse of the trapped warmth.

An emaciated fog is guarded by a slice of moon.

The rain is born sharp and dies with the caress of a pauper's hand.

It is so long since my skin has been touched that the reiteration of its existence surprises me. The drops are cold, but not unfriendly, as if the air is awake and would will all to wake with it.

Rain always sounds like something else. My particular journey's end is serenaded thus: water pouring from the sky like the clapping of small hands.

It applauds itself into my eyes and down my face and into my mouth, which is open to the elements.

I do not have a hat, but am sure I did once.

I cannot remember where I left it.

I lick the water off my lips. It tastes, oddly, like me.

I hear the floor creak, a young voice call out, but I do not recognise its source.

A door slams.

Then, I hear my father's voice call out with irritation: why does no one answer the door? The sound of it slaps into me with a feeling that has lain dormant for so long, it takes me a moment to recognise it.

I do not hear anyone reply. I think I hear my father sigh in exasperation and fling a book on a table, but cannot be definite.

London is so quiet and cold. The carriages on Suffolk Street sound muffled.

I see a small cat shiver.

I did not hear a thing on my way here, but witnessed enough to satisfy my curiosity. I had forgotten the golden light of London houses, and how it spills across roads like hysterical watercolours. I had forgotten how the intimation of fire hovers at the edge of houses. I had forgotten how thickly and quickly the coal dust settles on a shirtsleeve, and how the trees twist and moan at their lack of warmth. I had forgotten that birds could look miserable. I had forgotten the armies of damp beggars, and the extent of their deprivation.

I had forgotten how foul the streets are, even when washed clean with the elements.

At the instant that I pull the bell, a fancy coach pursuing a pair of fine greys flies past at such a speed the details of its journey are indistinct. One of the horses cries out and stumbles. The coachman whips and curses it, his fury wrapped in cloth.

A woman's laughter erupts from nowhere.

The poor beast throws me a supplicating glance, and they are gone.

I utter a stern prayer on the poor animal's behalf.

A man who would beat a horse is not worthy of the name of man.

My father opens the door. He has no knowledge of the date or time of my return.

Has it come to this, that my father should answer his own door?

Although I know it is dark, I do not realise I am in the shadows.

He looks about, perplexed. I am made suddenly aware of my invisibility, and emerge into the shining doorway and blink. He looks at me, calls out with a look of confusion, hello? and then stops his words as suddenly as if someone had popped a cork in his throat.

His face crumples like a failed drawing.

I look at him. He does not look as he did a year earlier.

I have been gone a lifetime and become a ghost. Can he see me as I see him?

He runs his fingers through his hair and gazes at me, as if I am no longer me, but a stranger. Only then does he confirm that the reality of this apparition is I.

No. Oh, Richard!

He wraps himself around my poor body, and holds me so tight that for a moment I forget to breathe. He moves my hand up and down like a woman desperate for water from a pump. I drop my suitcase onto the sidewalk and hear a corner shatter. My soft bag slides off my shoulders, pencils rattling, unheeded.

I arrive as laden as a mule and as willing.

I am undone.

You are so wet, my boy. My dear boy. My boy. I had no idea, why did you not contact us, and tell us of your arrival?

He talks to my hair and holds me close, as if he would banish the rain with his own warmth.

The darkness recedes for a moment. I am home. I am startled at the sound of a deep sob that I recognise, with surprise, as my own.

I force myself to pull away from the heat with the reluctance of a traveller leaving a fire on a wet night. I cannot look any longer into the face of this father of mine that has altered its shape in such subtle and strange ways.

The mouth, smaller. The eyes, less direct. The arms, larger.

While I am considering him, and he, me, as if from nowhere, for I did not hear them coming, all manner of arms reach out to touch me, surround me, hold me, imprison me. Faces like glowing saucers circle me like planets. Shining eyes bore into my own. My face is buried in sweet-smelling hair, and the voices of the girls toll high and joyful.

I taste tears on my lips. My knees wobble in exhaustion. I cannot feel my cold feet.

Names begin to attach to faces.

John Alfred, at least a league taller, his mouth still open, his eyes still gazing.

Richard! he cries.

Arthur John, shaking my hand like a man, and, also like a man, unable to look into my eyes.

Sarah, unaccountably weeping and holding her face in her handkerchief.

Richard, we did not know. We did not know where you were.

I do not know who utters these words, but they affect me in a way I do not immediately understand.

Where am I? Where was I?

Jane, smiling and patting my arm, father laughing and crying and talking and asking questions to break a traveller's heart. Everyone throwing words at me, as if I am a dancer and their words, violets. But beside us all, separate from the mayhem, a still, dark figure, twisting her hands, her face focussed on mine like a telescope on a star.

Oh Maria.

She takes my hand simply in hers, and it sits there, quiet. It is so cool and thin I cannot recognise it.

Surely, when I left, she had the chubby fingers of a child.

She is silent, and stands with her head drooping. A still pool amidst a hurricane. She looks at me and speaks.

Richard, come inside. It is raining.

Without another word, she leads me home, holding my hand so tightly I can feel every bone. She will not let me go.

Grass

Dim London rooms force me to walk in parks.

I walk between flowerbeds and beyond the silver ponds and through the long, thin grass, towards what? I do not know what, or who, I will meet, although feel clearly that I do know where I am going, despite my ignorance of my destination.

Trees move towards me slowly in the breeze.

Conversations crowd my mind.

Lucky birds float over my head.

I no longer know what is hidden, a fact that has ceased to worry me, for I do believe the world chooses well in what it lets me know.

I hold my face up to the sky and it falls towards me, relieved to find a friend.

Everything that exists whispers to me.

Our lives lack air. We spend too many hours indoors, our skin growing paler by the second, and then have the temerity to complain about eternity in a box.

I have begged my brothers and sisters to run through the rain, and embrace the cold wet air on their skin, but they turn away from me, their faces no longer the faces I knew, their voices the voices of others.

They long for stories of my travels, which I cannot supply. Nothing happened to me that was a story.

They are too resistant to understanding how dearly I hold their well-being in my heart. They will not accept that stories no longer exist for me, that everything that fills the earth and sky exists for a reason.

However, despite their unfamiliar appearances, the souls of my family are knit into my skin and into my heart, and keep me warm.

Why they resist my advice, I have yet to discover. But I will. It should not be difficult, simply a matter, as with all things, of observation.

But I do feel compelled, nonetheless, to ask in the strongest terms possible, what kind of a life it is when a man or a woman or a child is deprived access to the sky? What kind of a life is it when a man is starved of sun? What kind of an existence prostitutes goodness, and invites the devil to dinner?

We all wear black in our family now. Father says it facilitates the cleaning of coal dust off cloth, but in truth I feel it is because we are in mourning, constantly present at the wake of our dreams.

This sadness would be intolerable if I did not know that the sun is always present, even at night, somewhere.

The world is full to overflowing.

Nourishment

I dreamt I ate an owl last night. Sliced.

It called to me, and shivered. Its feathers shone in the soft night-light, and it called to me again, but I refused to listen to it and carved it so thin it was almost transparent.

It was served to me on a plate garnished with flowers. I do not remember who brought it to me.

A disgusting dream. I was glad, for once, to wake and indulge in the only meal I consider bearable.

After much experimentation I have narrowed it down to two delicious things, both enough to sustain a man, and both, in their own way, the correct ingredients for a truth-seeking man to swallow.

I eat chicken eggs, and sip ale. A belly full of thwarted birth and bubbles! A mind tickled with hops!

A fine meal, a perfect meal, one impossible to finish even when the food has gone. There is nothing more perfect than a cold white egg. An object with no beginning, and no edge. An infinite thing, a pure thing. Who could not be inspired to dream of warm golden fields and hot summer suns, eating eggs and drinking ale?

The hoppickers' fingers, flying brown and warm down the lines of hops, most decent of plants. A girl with red cheeks and clean hair, a basket on her arm, plucking eggs from the warmth of the nest, product of the kind chicken.

This is food and drink to nourish more than stomach.

A fine meal, a perfect meal, one impossible to finish even when the food has gone. Eggshells and amber glass pile up against the walls, still lives to digest even when the hunger has been satisfied.

Playthings for light, objects born again with every rare ray of sunshine. Bottles guard the soft pink excesses of eggshells which decorate my rooms; air, however dim or sad, hits their curves with a variation my imagination never tires of.

My castle is growing from the safest and most mysterious of bricks.

A Visit

My friends no longer come to the rooms I have taken to escape the intolerable demands of my so-called family, and I do not ask them why, but I do not care, involved as I am in making my first painting since returning to England. I have concentrated on rendering a scene of a group of water-carriers on the shore at Fortuna, near Mount Carmel. I will call it *Caravan Halted by the Seashore*. To once again have the luxury of paint and canvas at my disposal gives me greater joy than I could have imagined. Creating this image has occupied my mind to the point of distraction.

Surprisingly, however, a girl calling herself my sister Maria came through my door today, the words falling from her mouth as suddenly as her hat from her head, which she dropped without a glance on the floor.

It was a plain hat, and not bright.

At first I did not recognise her and looked at her face long and hard, to dissect her disguise.

She was at once as familiar to me as my own hands and a stranger. It was unnerving.

Without preamble she launched straight into what she had to say.

Richard, please, I want you to listen to me. Are you listening, Richard?

The girl was well informed.

I looked over her head. My room was very still.

My sister (delivered sarcastically), there is no one else here I could possibly listen to but you.

I meant the observation lightly, as an acknowledgement of our mutual masquerade, but she did not seem to hear the humour in my voice. Her lips came together in a wrinkled worried line, while her eyes shone hard and false at my own.

She was dressed in blue, and was thin. Her eyes were strange, holes in her head.

Richard, please. I want to talk with you quietly. I need you to listen to me.

I need your full concentration.

She then began to pull her handkerchief to bits. It was a mesmerising sight. It is difficult to tear cloth, and requires much strength, but this girl did not look strong.

I refused, however, to be distracted by such petty details, and so, despite the destruction of her haberdashery, I stood my ground.

I told her that nothing she could say to me could possibly interest me. Why should I rest in the middle of the day, when there are paintings to be made and thoughts to be thought?

People increasingly request the strangest things of me.

To know whom to welcome into my home is becoming more and more fraught.

Suddenly weary, I decided to sit down, to lend a polite ear to her falsehoods, to understand their provenance all the more clearly. However, an abrupt hammering on the door startled me and so, like any man whose door is hammered upon, I leapt up, confused as to who the identity of the person might be.

The girl attempted to intercept my investigation, so I was forced to whisper my reproach as fiercely as a whisper will allow.

Girl, are you expecting someone? Did someone escort you here?

I was convinced the hammering and this strange girl must somehow be linked. The coincidence was too great.

The thought must have frightened her, as her eyes filled with tears so bright her face was immediately covered in terrified diamonds.

Richard, it was only the footsteps of the lodger above. It is no one. It is nothing. There is no one at your door. They have left. Did you hear that, Richard, the door has slammed downstairs? There is no one there.

So does a woman deliver her sentence of deceit! With a jewelled face and reassuring words! How could she pretend not to hear the person who hammered so cruelly on my door? And she, supposedly my sister, my kin, my protector.

Impostor.

I suddenly realised that I had been listening so intently for the entrance of this stranger at my door, whose presence was so demanding of my energy and concentration, that I did not, at first, register the meaning of what this Maria was saying to me, but in a flash, it struck me as solidly as that unknown fist upon my door struck my eardrums.

She was trying to prevent me feeling what I know I have to feel. She would prefer I slept the sleep of the ignorant or intemperate than live as clearly as I can. She would prefer me docile to wise.

Despite my transparent disgust, she refused to be quiet. Words flew from her mouth like pistol-shots.

Richard, lie down, please. I want to talk with you, quietly. You are tired and need to rest. I have brought you some food. I will prepare it for you. Rest, Richard. Please, there is no one there.

She still spoke to me as if I were an invalid! Lie Down! Food! Rest!

Her hands took hold of my own and burnt me. I pulled them away. Her heat was infectious.

Let me make you some tea. Please Richard, some hot tea. Richard, you have not been eating properly. You need to eat. I will feed you.

Tea! A dull brown drink for sickly throats! Food! Banish the thought. Stuff for gluttons.

I did not dignify either her question or her observation with a reply.

I am filled with a fuel that propels me through the world with more energy than I should ever have thought possible. As if it were I who needed rest or nourishment!

Her sly hands came towards me again in a terrible, untruthful gesture of reconciliation. They clearly were shaking.

I pushed her away and could not look in her diamond eyes lest the truth of her betrayal be too clear even for my compassion.

I spoke above her head, to the wall.

Tell me where my father is, and perhaps I will talk with you.

A shriek from her and then a fist rammed into her mouth.

She spoke through her fingers.

Richard, you must stop this. Father is where he always is. At home. At work. With friends, all of whom you know.

She is such a liar it makes me breathless. I obviously cannot speak with her and so, instead, I looked from the window, up at the clouds whose shapes I endlessly play with in my mind's eye. The transfigured sky thrusts ideas in my mind so constantly I have begun to think of it as my apprentice.

I had become absorbed in watching a baby emerge fully clothed from behind a storm cloud and could feel the sun struggling to push the blanketed clouds away from its radiance, when I was pulled back to earth by the girl's howling, which I do believe she felt would convince me of her true identity. What comedy such deceit lends itself to. This actress playing my beloved sister had lost her lines! And who did she feel was best equipped to help her find them? Why, me! The situation was so absurd, all I could do was laugh and laugh, which, for reasons unknown to me, seemed to replenish the water supply of her tears. Her strange duplicity might be beguiling if it weren't so repulsive.

I hold my knowledge close to my heart, as it is the only dagger I know that will protect me well. I have learnt to identify the real skin beneath the surface. Whoever this girl is, she will never know as much as me.

The Beginnings of a Plan

So, I must plan the most appropriate strategy for doing battle with the devil, whom I will fight. Apathy is a powerful enemy. I will not be lulled into a false sense of security, even if he refuses to fight.

It is common knowledge that the devil can transform himself into any shape he wishes and is most enamoured of the ones we assume to be good. Some recent examples: I have witnessed teacups rattle with horror. I have seen the mouths of puppies froth. I have seen the eyes of children radiate a hot, hard wrong. I have seen my own family replaced by impostors, who I have been impelled to paint with their punishment meted out.

It has become increasingly apparent to me that the most evil of intentions can be hidden in the creases of the cup of a soft hand, in the vowels or syllables of a kind word, or in the faces of people we assume to love. After all, the devil follows the logic of men, and who are we more likely to trust? The people we know, or strangers we pass on the street?

Thus, I have built a suit of armour tight around my heart, and will use only my head to judge the righteousness of a situation.

It is possible I shall not find any adversaries yet, but I do know they are there. The only information I am now lacking is their names, not necessarily the ones they utter as their own, but the ones that have labelled their hearts.

I will not be swayed by what is superficially familiar.

Soft tongues will not move me.

Oh, the joy, after travelling for so long, to know with certainty what is right and what is not, causes my heart to relax. I am, at last, arriving at the home I have built from my own bricks, and it is not the one I once knew.

It is apt that the only words I own to express this new state of affairs appear as drawings fine as cobwebs. However, I am doubly lucky that if my clarity falters, a host of advice will immediately, and generously unsummoned, pour into my mind and ears, sourced directly, I am convinced, from the pure intentions of Osiris himself. It is enough luck to make a man whistle in the dark.

A Visit to a Doctor

We walk so quickly down a crowded street I stumble like a hack with splinters.

The man calling himself my father would take me by the hand if I would allow it.

(Where is my father? Where has my father gone?)

However, my fingers resist, and curl into a tight fist, so he clings instead to my coat sleeve.

I attempt to shake him off, but he persists.

It is quite astonishingly irritating. An image occurs to me: a gnat on the back of an elephant.

I giggle.

Beads of sweat tremble on his upper lip. His eyes are quite unnaturally large, and focussed on some unseen point he insists we rush towards. He has demanded I accompany him to visit a doctor, a Richard Sutherland, and I, for one, am too curious about what it all means to refuse.

I do not understand this preoccupation of people, none of whom I know, with the state of my health. They are constantly knocking on my door, or feeling my head, or bringing me idiotic, supposedly tasty morsels of food, or lapsing, in the middle of dull conversations, into silences fraught with a meaning I cannot fathom.

I do not understand it, not in the least. I have never felt

more powerful or well, and they treat me as if I were a sickly child knocking on the gates of heaven.

We hurry along a street I do not recognise, dodging faces I have never seen. Puffing, this father speaks to me in thin vowels, like a man with a dry mouth.

Richard, he will help you. I promise you, Richard, he is a good man. He is a modern man.

Ah, once again, the problem of the good man. The man the whole world might support, and in their ignorance, support wrongly.

Father, (oh words heavy with humour), Father, I cannot support you in your assumption. I do not know his heart. He does not know mine. How can a man help someone of whose heart he has no knowledge? And how can a man who has no knowledge of the helper's heart, accept such help? The conditions are unclear. No one in their right mind would accept them.

The man hurrying so quickly at my side throws his head back, follows the clouds with his eyes, and does not reply. He does, however, give his lips a little lick.

If his response accords me a certain amount of satisfaction I do not reveal it, but allow that his silence acknowledges my small victory. A modern man! Oh, foolish man calling himself my father.

(Where is my father? Where has my father gone?)

This is not the way to endear this so-called doctor, to me. I want to shout, what was so failed in the ancients that needed to be substituted with such flimsy falsehoods?

I cannot think of one instance that might justify such substitution.

What is there in the modern world that did not exist in the ancient one?

What, in heaven's name, was in need of improvement, apart from the ever-present fundamental of men learning to recognise the truth? Nothing. Nothing has changed, but the design of clothes and bricks and paltry flesh.

And they, for one, are easy to discard.

The End, Again

Sometimes it is appropriate to speak dishonestly, if only to lure the dishonest closer to the net of their maker, whose responsibility it will then be to cast a cleanliness around untruth.

This is a man I do not know, but who calls himself my father.

(Where is my father? Where has my father gone?)

I would give anything to have my real father back, but cannot find him until this charlatan is disposed of.

To build a new house you have to pull down the bricks of the old dwelling. Sometimes the bricks shriek as they are torn down, but who would heed the cry of rotten bricks?

I cannot let such cries bleed into my brain and distort the truth, the truth that has solid, if seemingly invisible, foundations.

This man calling himself my father, he is not my father.

There is nothing to be done but to strip away the disguise he has so cunningly built, and so reveal the good, the clean, and the real foundations of what we so easily call the truth.

And so I tell him I must speak with him, at a place we both know.

He has done his research well, and recognises the place I mention as one my father, my real father, would respond to.

I tell him that once there, I will explain my motivations.

I tell him I am nostalgic for my childhood. I inform him, in clear tones, that I will clarify for him the situations that I have immersed myself in, the ones that confuse him. I tell him that, once there, he will understand. I tell him that in the pure country air, all will become clear.

I tell him that I need to escape the filth of London, if only for a night or two.

I tell him I need fresh air and clarity and communication.

I tell him I must unburden my mind.

I tell him I love him.

And so we travel to Cobham, site of childhood happiness.

We travel together, and laugh.

We move towards his destination and he is happy, believing us to be close.

He has become so happy his face softens at the edges.

He relaxes and links his arm through mine.

He thinks he has earned my trust.

When we arrive we are hungry from our travels.

We find beds for the night and stroll to The Ship Inn, where we eat our fill, and drink to ease our communication. Men laugh as they drink in the rich light.

I cannot hear their words but only see the shape of their mouths as they utter their meaningless sounds.

The sound of a cuckoo conveys more sense to me now.

Our bellies are full and warm and we grow quiet with indulgence.

The father impostor stretches, yawns, smiles at me, and suggests we should sleep, it is late.

I inform him that I would like to walk to places we once loved. I tell him the night air is a tonic. I suggest, gently, that a walk will help me rest, will calm my nerves.

He is generous and listens to my request, and so, into the night, we walk.

The sky, the air and the ground, all are dark and cold. The roads are empty.

Sleeping birds wake at our footsteps and cry out.

How can a bird know that the morning will come?

Words drop from our mouths, fade, and then stop.

I embrace the silence with a joyful heart.

This man beside me shivers and attempts to hide it. He wraps his coat around him, and ignorantly talks of tomorrow. He takes a large white handkerchief from his pocket and noisily blows his nose.

We walk towards water, which mirrors the moonlight.

He looks at me, and does not understand.

How could he?

Suddenly, and with immense clarity, I know the moment has come to act.

Everything in me converges.

And so I take my blade and without warning I strike him, to propel him towards his maker who knows more than I.

I am simply the messenger.

At first it is as if nothing has happened. Everything is still. The sky. Flesh. Mouths.

I am all eyes. My hands are linked to my sight. My heart has disappeared.

The man is astonished. His mouth opens but he makes no sound. He stares at me with bewilderment and looks down. My eyes follow his hands that he presses to his side. Then he moans, but still, we do not move.

We are as expectant as men waiting for a train.

For a moment, his clothes are the same as they ever were, and then they are not. His dull black coat is suddenly stained with a wet dark brown.

I think of a newly painted door. Or mud.

The colour of his face is not as it was. It is very pale, yet hot.

He moans once more and looks at me with eyes that slowly slip.

His body falls to one side and then stumbles. I hold my arms out and hold him tight so he cannot leave.

For a few seconds we are quiet together.

He whispers, please, Richard.

He is so corrupted he does not comprehend the magnitude of his untruthfulness.

Then the stillness is no longer and I am filled with fury and my heart is back where it belongs. I plunge my good clean knife into this impostor's throat. He must not be allowed to breathe a minute longer. His violent hands push me away then return to clutch at his neck.

My blade drags through his skin, which is thick and difficult to cut.

I summon all of my strength.

I pull the blade out and push it in again and again, and then slice this man from side to side.

His flesh creaks and splits. His skin bursts and then deflates.

He has become something other than himself.

He makes noises that I have never heard before. Gargling like someone drowning, but still breathing.

I remember walking on beaches beneath the sun and crushing thin shells with my boots.

I remember a woman gutting fish and whistling.

I recall hot poultices exploding boils.

I remember my father.

The memory inspires my power and my fury.

This man does not receive my message well and argues with all of his dwindling strength.

His arms move up and down as they attempt to push me away. His fingers drum my face. His legs scrabble to escape and then crumple.

A bird shrieks, the water shimmers. Mud grips the soles of my boots and I slip but hold onto him all the more tightly.

He begs and begs. He bleeds, he shrieks. He faintly cries.

He chokes on my name like a spell that would save him.

And then he fades.

My hands are red, his face is red, the mud is red.

Everything sticks to everything else.

Skin separates skin.

Spittle hits my face, fingernails have torn my flesh.

I too am bleeding.

It is distasteful.

Why should a man struggle at such a simple introduction to his maker?

I strip the mask from his throat and eyes and then finally he is peaceful.

The confusion in his eyes has gone forever.

From this moment on they will never deceive another soul.

He has departed into a hell of his own making and the person I once was has died.

And so, it is also time for me to leave, but to a different destination. I move towards the light.

It is time to find my father.

Broadmoor Hospital, 1885

All men live in shells yet dead souls float upwards, into the light.

It is so much more difficult to live than to die.

I will welcome the weightlessness of death, when the time comes for it to claim me.

I believe it will be soon.

My father has never visited me here, except when I sleep.

Occasionally I wake with the imprint of his warm hand on my brow.

Maria has long gone. My sister refused to understand what it was I had to do, even though she, too, was impersonated.

My brothers, my sisters, my family have forsaken me.

God knows where they are.

Without the consolation of spirits I would be no one.

My one responsibility here has been to paint the visitations of beings whose role it is to supply solace to lost souls.

I have been obliged to reveal the tangled meaning of surfaces.

I have clarified distant memories of travelling through heat, escorted by the sun.

I have spent many hours exploring the complex exterior of leaves, and the reflections that inhabit the heart of water.

I have painted the important marriages of mythology and the underworld souls who have lent me such respite.

I have painted portraits of my friends.

I have painted the world that lives inside this one.

My brush is never still.

My pencil flies over paper on a journey more infinite than any I have ever taken.

Paint has become my canopy.

I will be joining my father soon and the thought of it fills me with joy.

I do not know where it was he went, but am sure I will be able to find him. We will exist in harmony, I have no doubt about that. We will become members of a great community of souls enclosed in walls of air and comforted by the sun.

I know my father will be the first to thank me for liberating him from that impostor.

In all modesty, it will be good, finally, to be thanked.

But sometimes when I wake, I wonder, where did I come from to arrive at this place?

A hospital. A place for the sick, yet I have never had a single day of illness in my life.

My flesh, perhaps, has been weak, but my soul overflows with rude good health.

It rains so much my bones are damp and will not dry.

When I die once more, my bones will dry in light.

Perhaps the story chooses the man and wraps him in it until he suffocates.

For me, the sun made up my mind, and the sun became my story.

But what of before?

Sometimes when I wake, I wonder, where did I come from to arrive at this place?

Acknowledgments

Thank you to Verso for reissuing *Bedlam* and to everyone on the team there.

Thank you to my agent, David Godwin.

Thank you to Paul Allatson for publishing an earlier version of *Bedlam* – then titled *Son* – in the University of Technology Sydney ePress journal *PORTAL* in 2004.

Thank you to Sternberg Press in Berlin for publishing *Bedlam* in 2006.

Thank you, as ever, to my friends and family – my ballast.

Bedlam was inspired by Richard Dadd's extraordinary paintings, which I first saw in the exhibition Victorian Fairy Painting at the Royal Academy of Art in London in 1998. During the writing of this novel, I found Patricia Allderidge's *The Late Richard Dadd, 1817–1886* (1974), published by Tate Gallery, invaluable.

Whilst many of the events I write about did happen in some form or other, *Bedlam* is fundamentally a work of imagination.